The Distant Eye

A novel by

Paul Tausch

ISBN: 1-4392-5936-4
ISBN-13: 9781439259368
Library of Congress Control Number: 2009909813

To Tristan Hans Tausch,
a longer-than-usual bedtime story.
Dad

Foreword

The Distant Eye started as a manga for my son, Tristan. Originally intended as a few pages of drawings with a handful of text, it became clear to me that parts of the story needed more development. I sat down to add some additional descriptive text to develop the Order of the Celestial Lotus in more detail, as well as to create some intentionally vague elements relating to the possible origin of Möbius, and I was quickly over a hundred pages!

The environment in the story is nebulous, allowing all of the focus to fall onto the characters and their situation. No extraneous adults or daily responsibilities seem to hinder these youthful characters; they all appear to have been raised as amazingly self-sufficient, responsible individuals. If this is starting to sound Utopian, it is just that, until the antagonist appears on the scene.

While written for a creative, well-read nine-year old, the story itself serves as a reflection on the importance of intelligence, character, and perseverance in addressing seemingly impossible situations. I could not resist utilizing at least the appearance of one of my favorite Greek literary devices, *deus ex machina*, although at the same time giving the reader an insight to the real mechanics behind the scene (or in a parallel dimension, as it were).

A special thanks to Kim — my editor, biggest supporter, and best friend, who also happens to be my lovely wife!

I now hope to return to my original thought of continuing this story via a manga production for as long as it may hold Tristan's interest, but hope that he always falls back on this story, if for no other reason than to know I loved the time we spent reading together and creating our own stories filled with imaginative creatures.

CHAPTER ONE
(The Beginning)

Jukka Hendriksson and the seven members of his search team arrived at the base camp hours after the last sunlight had faded. The basin was peppered with russet canvas tents glowing from the buttery warmth of the kerosene lanterns within. One of the larger barracks was prepared for Jukka's team.

There were three large search parties that had been scouring the mountain range on a search and rescue mission for almost four days, trying desperately to find the hunting party from their village that had been lost now for over two weeks. Among the hunters were friends, neighbors, loved ones, and most notably, the magistrate of the village.

Jukka Hendriksson was leading a team that consisted of seven seasoned climbers and hunters. There were forty men in total among all three of the search parties. Every one of the forty had some association with at least one of those that were currently missing.

The mountain that they searched (and searched was an understatement; no stone in the areas they had covered remained unturned or niche un-checked) was named the Zeitlos-Granit. This peak was in many ways as much a part of Jukka's village as even the oldest surviving elder alive today. The shelter provided by this mountain had brought the village of Orneth into existence—given it birth as the countless mothers living there since had birthed the generations that populated the history of this village.

Zeitlos-Granit gave life by pouring forth crystal-clear snow melt into the village for the purest water, by embracing a wide open expanse of land for livestock to graze, and by serving as a natural barrier between the mild climate of Orneth from the harshness of the arid lands to the south. On occasion, though, the mountain also reclaimed life. Everyone sincerely hoped that this was not a case of the latter.

Each of the three teams had defined an area on the mountain that they would search and had agreed to meet back on this day at this spot to set up a base camp and reassess their efforts. It had been everyone's sincerest hope that one of the groups would return with the entire hunting party safely in tow.

The moon was already bright white and large in the blue-black sky, giving the whole camp a surreal glow. The soft light illuminated objects in the camp and created a stark contrast with the surrounding darkness; Jukka observed how the night filtered out much of the background and actually made certain things easier to see than during broad daylight. A jagged swath of darkness tore into the glowing orb above as the moon passed behind the Zeitlos on its course into the nighttime sky. The cold, harsh peak of the granite mountain blocked out a portion of the moonlight and appeared as a feral claw tearing at the ethereal body, trying to keep it from attaining its rightful place.

Jukka stopped and stared at this mean profile in silent respect. The moon's surface shimmered like a white sand desert in contrast to the dark peak that stood before it in defiance.

This mountain had claimed more men then he cared to remember, and he stood firmly prepared to once again fight for those currently lost. The Zeitlos was like a sleeping giant once again awakened by these hapless interlopers; the mountain could only tolerate so many trespassers over the years before it finally lost patience with their intrusion and lashed out in exasperation.

Breaking from his bleak reverence, Jukka continued on, moving farther into the camp. He heard his men following closely behind, talking in tired voices.

Clusters of men sat by open campfires outside, sipping strong, dark coffee and talking about the events of the day while listening for the call to dinner. Every one of these waiting men jumped to their feet and waved to Jukka and his group, looking anxiously for faces from the lost hunting party mixed in with Jukka's team or for some sign that they had found a trace of the lost men—anything that proffered hope, anything that would make their mission a success.

"No success today, Jukka?" a younger man asked as he moved beside the older man. Coffee sloshed and spilled out from the tin mug he carried.

"No failure, either," Jukka replied. "Tomorrow gives us another chance."

Jukka's team had been equally hopeful that they would arrive to boisterous cheers and good news at the base camp. They were quickly disappointed; it was clear from these expectant faces that there would be no celebration tonight.

Jukka sighed and swung the pack off of his back. He propped it against an empty tent and walked toward the center of the camp. The two individual flags of the other teams were already flying, telling him that his was the last of the three teams to arrive. One of his team would retrieve their green flag from Jukka's pack and hoist it up the flagpole while he went on to meet with the other team leaders, who would already be waiting for him.

Stretching his arms wide and rocking back and forth to loosen his sore back muscles, he heard the familiar snaps and pops of his bones. Jukka bent down to sweep some of the trail dust off of his rough leather hiking trousers. As the dust floated away in clouds, the deep forest green color of the leather shone through. Straining further, he reached down and removed a small cluster of some silvery brush that had been hitchhiking in the laces of his calf-high mountain climbing boots.

"I have a bad feeling about this search expedition."

Jukka jerked his head to the left. A cloud of smoke was illuminated in the shadows by the deep orange glow of a pipe. The face beyond was indiscernible.

"Well, friend," Jukka replied slowly, straining to figure out the identity of the speaker. "The fact that we're searching for lost souls is no reason to celebrate. And sometimes how we *feel* about something has very little to do with anything at all."

The hidden man took a deep drag on the pipe, and the glow from the burning tobacco created a disturbing, boorish mask on the smoker. Deep shadows on the unshaven face hid the eyes; the light made the cheeks and nose seem sharp and pronounced. The image reminded Jukka of a kabuki performance he had seen depicted in a book when he was a child. It had disturbed him then, and seeing it engulfed in rings of smoke and speaking in such an ominous manner brought those disturbing memories back once again.

"Besides," Jukka continued, more to break the awkward silence than to further engage in conversation, "that means there is still hope."

"I do not believe there is any hope in this situation. I believe that you know this will end badly."

The voice sounded vindictive, and despite the discomfort of the situation, Jukka's anger was starting to flare at this naysayer's words.

Jukka found that he was crouching and leaning toward the smoking shadow, trying to get a closer look.

"Jukka! Everyone's waiting," a voice echoed from the end of the corridor. Jukka waved to the figure in the distance.

Straightening himself to stand upright, he turned to have the last word with this dark, cynical figure. Only a fading cloud of smoke lingered.

Jukka continued down the wide thoroughfare through the camp, agitated at this strange encounter. Emerging from a row of smartly constructed tents and neatly stacked supplies, Jukka saw a group of men huddled beneath a large cloth canopy at the center of the open grassy vale. Goats were common at this elevation, and several sizzled on spits over two large, open fire pits that had been dug in the ground. Black cast iron kettles frothed and bubbled, the heavy aroma of the cabbage, potatoes, and peppers from inside mingling with that of the goats to create a smorgasbord for the senses.

Dinner would be ready soon, and everyone would eat together. But first Jukka needed to talk with the other team leaders. He knew no one had been successful today, and he was anxious to discuss the plans for tomorrow.

Jukka Hendriksson had come to Orneth from the Ice Land as a young boy. Tall as a youth, he had grown into an even taller man and one of the most skilled mountain climbers in Orneth. Now almost seventy, Jukka still towered over most of the men here and was probably in better physical condition than almost all. Everyone here enjoyed the stories Jukka passed on from his relatives in the Ice Land, stories of how they would trek the ice fields for days or how they had spent weeks climbing to the top of the volcano there and then hiked down through the vents into some of the most beautiful and amazing caverns below. One particular ancestor, generations back in the eighteenth or nineteenth century Jukka recalled, told of acting as a guide and entertaining a curious French writer one summer. He described how his relative ended up serving as a model for a character in the science fiction novel that this French fellow wrote about traveling into those very caverns. Jukka couldn't say for sure if that was true, but it made for a fine story nonetheless.

Because of his height, Jukka had to bend down to enter the canopy. He had to stoop even farther because of his hat, which still brushed against the undulating brown canvas border encircling the canopy. The other two team leaders stood and shook hands with Jukka as he stepped into the light and warmth of the canopy, and someone else handed him a tin mug of steaming black coffee. Everyone said their hellos and then made their way back to the large table at the center of the awning. News had already traveled through the camp that Jukka's team had found nothing either.

Lanterns glowed brightly around the awning, suspended by short climbing ropes with carabineers at each end. Jukka's pale blue eyes sparkled in the warm yellow light of the lanterns. His leathery skin was tan and wrinkled from countless days out in the sun, exposed to the harsh elements. White stubble covered his face from having gone several days without shaving, and unruly strands of white hair showed from beneath the large green felt fedora he now almost always wore when outside. A tuft of animal hair bristled from a silver ring in the hatband, and a fur strap ran from each side of the hat and met under his chin to hold it in place against the strong breezes that made their home where Jukka liked to climb.

A large map of the Zeitlos-Granit was spread out on the central table. Hand-painted onto a sheet of soft pale leather, the map itself was both handsome and old. Combinations of rich sienna and burnt umber beautifully mingled across the sheepskin to depict the mountain range, flanked by abundant fields of verdant foliage. A swath of deep cerulean blue dipped down from the northeast right corner to represent the southern tip of the Dark Sea.

Jukka had seen this map many times displayed within the city hall back in Orneth. Each time he saw it, he remarked that it was truly a work of art in both its design and accuracy.

"We've just finished mapping out where our groups covered, Jukka," a voice from the crowd confirmed what he saw in front of him. Yellow and red pushpins peppered the map, radiating outward from the large black pin that represented the base camp in which they now stood.

"We saved the green pins for you, Jukka."

In a subconscious movement, Jukka removed his pince-nez from his breast pocket and perched the spectacles upon the bridge of his nose. The gold wire that held the lenses in place shone brightly, polished from years of being transported inside of a fleece-lined pocket. His now-magnified eyes once again peered even more closely at the situation represented by these colorful pins. Swirls of pale blue and flecks of gold were coaxed out from behind these lenses by the array of lanterns scattered about.

Jukka reached over and took a handful of green pins from a ceramic container and commenced to place them in various points of an as yet untouched area, his tough leathery skin immune to the piercing shafts. These pins now represented the area of terrain that Jukka and his team had covered over the past three days.

The result of the three teams' efforts created a flower with three petals, each a different color, blooming over the rugged topography beneath. Gray shadows radiated outward onto the map from these pins and swayed softly in unison with the flames of the lanterns. These shadowy bars crossed and mingled across the mountain range beneath, appearing to the men who looked on as iron bars keeping those for whom they search locked within.

"We've covered quite a bit of territory between our three groups, Jukka," said Byron Coleman, the leader representing the yellow pins. "I can't imagine how a hunting party that size could have pushed farther than this before the storm hit. This has to be very close to the area where we saw all the lightning from that storm."

Everyone nodded in agreement, and a few "ayes" were heard.

"But we haven't found a single trace." Byron shook his head. He looked tired. Dark circles beneath his eyes emphasized the desperation in his voice.

Jukka thought back over the bizarre events that had brought him here to this base camp on the Zeitlos-Granit. He recalled just three weeks ago now, the quaint parade down the main thoroughfare of their small village that had sent the annual hunting party out with the best wishes of the town. He smiled as he thought of the hunters walking proudly down the main street in their fine hunting clothes, marshaled by their charismatic young magistrate. As this group waved to the crowds, the townspeople pelted them all lovingly with flowers and rice (the children actually hurled the rice at the procession like the hunters were the wild game! These little ones would gain the loving respect for this ceremony later in life, when they would begin to dream of being old enough to be part of this group as well). This was an annual ritual that celebrated the village's relationship with nature and meant far more to everyone involved than the value of the meat that the party would bring back. Jukka had been in the pageant many times throughout his life but would remain behind this year. He felt a pang of envy standing in the crowd throwing handfuls of rice.

Two days into the hunting trip, a freak storm front rolled in from the south without warning. Colossal banks of swollen dark clouds advanced swiftly across the clear sky and blocked the sun. People stood in wonder, watching as a dark line of storm clouds exploded ominously over the mountain range like an angry army battalion marching malevolently into battle, trampling the cobalt blue sky as it advanced. The pleasant warmth of the day had immediately become cold and damp, and the heavens had opened, dumping an unbelievable amount of rain.

Flood waters quickly saturated the soil and then, with nowhere else to go, poured across the land, relentlessly pounding Orneth and every village in its path with wall after wall of cold, dark water. Deep fissures appeared in the land, destroying roads and wiping out crops. Ranchers, unable to make it their pens and corrals in time, lost a great deal of livestock in the floods.

Even though the wind tore across the plains, driving the heavy dark clouds and rains before it, a spectacular electrical storm remained oddly stationary, confined over the Zeitlos. Fleeting pillars of orange fire could be seen rising up after a constant barrage of heavy lightning strikes, only to be quickly extinguished by the torrential rain. This terrifying display of nature's power went on for hours.

No one in Orneth, including Jukka, had ever seen a storm of such fury and power, and hoped to never see such a terrifying thing again. Jukka was relieved that his and his daughter's home had been relatively unscathed, avoiding any serious or irreparable damage. The flood waters had risen about knee deep in their interconnected homes, but the walls were thick and solid, and the foundation strong. When the waters receded, everything remained standing and intact—covered in mud, but intact.

The skies were clear and blue the next morning, and the people of Orneth thought the hunting party would certainly start their return home after such an intense and devastating storm the previous night.

Jukka had several times been up in the Zeitlos during heavy rains, and remembered one occasion where he had been caught in a flashflood up on the mountain. Everything had been dry and the sky veiled with only the thinnest of cloud covering, just enough to make for very pleasant hiking. He recalled the sky growing dark, followed by the rain descending quickly, just as it had for the magistrate's hunting party, but on a much smaller scale. Torrents of muddy water abruptly appeared and shot down the rugged chutes of granite, carrying with them tons of rich black topsoil and debris. To avoid drowning, he had lashed himself to a large outcropping of stones for fear of being washed away by the powerful deluge. Trees, brush, and several helpless ibex went streaming by, carried by the great force of the floods rushing down the mountain range.

Reaching out to try and free a small, bleating ibex kid tangled in a mass of debris near him, Jukka had been struck squarely in the side of the head by a large section of a log. He saw stars and had then blacked out for a brief time. Sputtering and choking, he regained consciousness with his face partially submerged in the roaring stream. With a severe headache, a large gash above his ear, and damp supplies, Jukka cut his journey short and made his way back down the muddy face of the mountain.

Many years had gone by since then, and Jukka tried to envision how the magistrate and his party would react in such a situation.

Several days passed after the horrific storm, and the town worked hard to clean up the refuse spread by the flood waters and began to repair the damage as they knew the magistrate would have wanted. Workers regularly glanced up toward the mountains, hoping to catch a glimpse of the party containing so many of their best men walking back toward town, but no one appeared.

Jukka worked like everyone else to try and restore order and clean up after the floods. Sorting through silt-covered belongings, washing the muck from their clothes and hanging them and the rugs they could salvage out to dry in the sun was keeping him very busy. Then came the larger projects, such as filling the gullies that now ran through the roads on his property and repairing downed fences, but he had a difficult time keeping his focus off of the mountain.

"I'm glad you stayed behind, Father," Jukka's daughter said one morning. He had guided this same expedition two years prior, and for many years before that, but had stayed home this time to spend time with his newest granddaughter and to help his own daughter around her home. Jukka had been widowed now for just over two years and spent as much time as possible with his daughters and granddaughters.

"I was just thinking that very same thought." Jukka smiled and hugged his daughter tightly.

What he did not say was that he was also wishing that he had gone with the party, feeling his presence might have improved their chance of survival. Such were the mixed emotions brought on by the onus of responsibility.

He knew the guide who had led the magistrate's party; Max Flemming was his name. He was known by all to be an excellent guide and climber with years of experience.

But after two weeks, when things were beginning to return to normal for most people, it became apparent that the hunters were not able to return home on their own. Jukka, along with the other two most seasoned climbers in Orneth, Byron Coleman and Karl Metzer, decided to assemble teams and head up to search for the party.

And now here he stood at a base camp with three complete search parties, having found absolutely nothing after almost four days. Once again up on the Zeitlos, Jukka prayed that they would be able to find all of these men. He knew the Zeitlos-Granit, like all mountains, could be ruthless and unforgiving to those who tempted fate and put themselves in the hands of such fickle elements. Mountains such as this on occasion granted fame to the few who conquered them, but they mostly took from the men unprepared and unwilling to give their all to survive the challenges of nature.

Stories that Jukka had heard since birth told that the Ark of Noah had come to rest somewhere in the aeries of the Zeitlos after the Great Flood, but no one had ever found a trace of the giant ship. Jukka often found himself daydreaming during his climbs that he would find the giant hull of gopher wood completely intact, resting peacefully in some hidden crevasse. With the effort that these three teams were putting in on this search, if the Ark were here, he was certain it would be found.

Jukka thought how truly terrible it would be if this mountain had claimed these men. Those below would live forever in the shadow of the mountain that had taken their loved ones. The Zeitlos would become a towering gravestone, a constant reminder of their loss if Jukka and the other search parties failed.

Now looking down at this map and calculating the square kilometers of ground they had covered in their initial three days, Jukka felt a pit forming in his stomach. The pins on the map represented a very large amount of territory. Jukka agreed with Byron that the search parties had trekked farther up into the Zeitlos than the magistrate and his party could have possibly traveled. Certainly three search parties moving with focus and purpose had covered more territory than a group of twelve men saddled with provisions and hunting gear. This estimation did not even consider that the searchers had been blessed with clear skies and had not been forced to flee from such an apocalyptic storm.

Not a single scrap of cloth, an extinguished campfire, or even a single shell casing was present anywhere. It was as if the men had never set foot on the Zeitlos-Granit.

"I wonder if they had not made it as far up onto the mountain before the storm hit as we estimate," Karl suggested. "Maybe they were in the lower steppes and cut down to the northeast to look for shelter on the opposite side. They could be somewhere over here," Karl said, tapping an area some distance from the cluster of pins.

Karl was trying to appear positive, and everyone appreciated his attempt, however inadequate.

"I've looked at our supplies for the red and yellow teams, and each group has enough supplies to last for about two days maximum. I think we had all expected to find our friends much sooner. I propose that we each head back toward Orneth, taking a long route back, heading down through these trails." Karl once tapped the area that he thought might have served as a safe haven for the magistrate's party. "I'll take this route; it will take longer than two days, but we can swing farther over to this small village. I know some folks who live there, and we can restock our supplies before getting back on this main road here." His finger traced a curving line on the map.

"That sound like a good plan," said Byron. "We'll do the same, but I'll follow a route directly north into this small canyon. We can then cut back across the base of the Zeitlos at the bridge right here."

"The magistrate and his party could have gotten completely disoriented in the weather and be almost anywhere, but I believe they would try to head down. These were really their only two choices; they obviously did not take the same path back toward Orneth that they took up onto the mountain," Karl said.

"I think we'll head farther up," Jukka spoke quietly. "Just to make sure; I think we'll all feel better knowing we exhausted every reasonable possibility.

"We won't go too much farther; I know my men are anxious to get back home to their families, as am I. My daughter was hoping I would be out for less than a week.

"If we're lucky enough to come across some wild game, we might stay out a few extra days. But we will definitely start our return within five days, no matter what."

Everyone nodded their heads in silence. They knew Jukka was right about trying every possibility to find the lost group. They all were beginning to fear the worst, but no one wanted to admit a loss of hope out loud.

"One week from now, we'll plan to see you back in Orneth, Jukka. No later," Byron said. "Don't make us come back up looking for you." He tried to say this in a light way, but his words were clearly heartfelt and sincere.

With that, Byron told the cooks to ring the dinner bell. As the welcomed and gentle tolling reached warmly out into the night, everyone dispersed back to their tents to grab their utensils for dinner.

Dried meats, fruits, and nuts had provided sustenance for the men, but after three days of hiking the mountain, they were all craving something more substantial and attacked the fresh, hot food with vigor. Jukka explained the plans to his men, and they ate with even more determination, in anticipation of the less-than-satisfying diet awaiting them over the next few days of continued searching. With full stomachs and aching muscles, everyone quickly drifted off after dinner, leaving the camp silent, except for occasional snores.

The next morning, many of the men were up and dressed long before the agreed-upon time for breakfast. While normally enjoying a few quiet and peaceful moments of warmth beneath a wool blanket on such a cool dark morning, today everyone was anxious to continue their search and had immediately sprang from bed upon waking.

Jukka's team set off toward the higher, more rugged regions of the Zeitlos-Granit. The dark granite peaks above were as familiar to Jukka as any of his old acquaintances, but he did not now consider them friends in any way.

After two days of hiking, they were well past the tree line, and the landscape was starkly different from the rolling green grasslands of the base camp. Barren and harsh, the panorama here was absent of any color beyond the flint gray of the stone and the black soil, which was still muddy and slick from the rains. A damp coldness set in, finding its way into the joints and backs of the members of the search party, reminding the older men of their age and generally making the going miserable.

Cresting a ridge, Jukka's team stopped abruptly. Spreading out before them, where a small peak should have risen to separate where they stood and the mountain top beyond, was a shallow crater. Jukka and his team stood dumbfounded. At first, Jukka thought he might be lost, that the landscape might have been altered by the rains, leading him to take a wrong turn. Stopping to think and scanning his surroundings, he knew that was not the case. Over the years, he and many of these men with him had traversed this area countless times, and there was no doubt that a rocky crest should be standing right in this spot.

Jukka's eyes followed the bed of the crater until it faded into the horizon, marveling at the size of the depression. Blackened and charred, he thought that a meteor had possibly struck here but quickly dismissed the thought; someone below in Orneth would have seen the path of a meteor massive enough to create this—not to mention that such an impact would have rocked Orneth and the whole of the area, probably causing avalanches and generally sending a massive amount of rock and dust into the sky. Piles of soggy refuse and stone would be scattered across a large area, but Jukka saw nothing extraordinary outside of the perimeter of the large depression, aside from the conditions caused by the water.

He and several of his men tentatively stepped down into the burnt crater. Their feet passed through the veil of ash that blanketed the ground, and continued into thick mire. Jukka looked down as he freed his foot and saw a brief shimmer as water trickled in to fill the void. He planted his feet and surveyed the area again. From this vantage point, it was clear that the entire floor of the crater was peppered with depressions like his footprint, only much larger.

Sniffing the air, an unpleasant smell permeated his senses; Jukka assumed this was the result of the ash and rain mixing to form lye.

Jukka saw a pile of rubble in the center of the crater and moved in that direction. His heart sank as he came upon the heap. Here lay the clues the search teams had been seeking. Here were the remnants for which they had searched and which Jukka wished now that they had not found.

He chided himself for being selfish. Their primary goal was of course to find the men alive. Second-best, it would be nice to keep the hope alive that the men were still alive; even lost meant they could someday still return. But these tell-tale signs said otherwise. This eerie scene would forever be ingrained in the memory of each member of Jukka's group. These images of this enigmatic crater would return frequently to haunt their sleep.

All of the supplies from the magistrate's hunting party were here. A small circle constructed of backpacks, sleeping bags, tents still in their cases, rocks, ice chests, and large chunks of burnt timber looked to have been quickly fashioned into some sort of makeshift stronghold or fort.

The gear was all clearly the property of the men from Orneth, with recognizable names labeled onto much of the camping gear. At about three-foot intervals around the entire circle, rifles pointed outward, resting on or against the incomplete perimeter wall. Piles of spent brass shell casings were built up by each rifle, littering the entire area. Hints of dull brass were visible all around, partially buried in the mud.

Empty boxes were scattered about; the colored inks that decorated the disintegrating fiberboard of the shell boxes were fading and smeared from saturation with water. A large canvas duffle containing a scant few decomposing ammunition cartons was torn to shreds. Looking inside, he saw these boxes were empty also. The men had been in such a hurry that they had removed the ammunition without even troubling to remove the paper boxes from the duffle. Jukka stared at the scene.

"They were in an awful hurry to get to those shells," one of his men commented as he stood beside Jukka and stared at the ripped duffle.

The zipper of the bag was still zipped; long tears ran through the cloth on either side.

The bulk of this haphazard citadel faced the direction from which Jukka's team had come up the mountain. Jukka loosened the fur band under his chin and removed his broad fedora, scratching his head. Maybe he had been thinking about this all wrong. He had focused on where the group was at the time of the storm, assuming that they would turn back as soon as the storm had subsided. Judging by the distance they had covered, it looked like the real trouble could have been after the storm, and that these men had been running *from* something, not toward shelter from the weather that had already subsided. Jukka had a sense that the location of this pile of gear represented the point of desperation, the point at which they could no longer stay ahead of whatever pursued them, and they had decided to make their stand and fight. Every round of ammunition they had carried for their entire trip had been spent here in a last-ditch effort for survival.

But against what?

There was not a single trace of the men themselves, though. One of Jukka's men captured photographic images of the scene before they began to dig through the rubble, searching for clues. One of the men commented that he felt like he was desecrating a grave by disturbing the scene, and Jukka could empathize but knew that they had a duty to those who remained in the village, waiting in anguish for these search teams to return with good news, to try and recover any and all personal articles of the fine men who had apparently perished here. He had found the clues that he had so desperately wanted, but the evidence he looked upon was far from what he had hoped for. Jukka had wanted to find the entire hunting party wandering lost on the mountain. If only to himself, it seemed he had to admit that they were lost forever.

Without thinking, Jukka reached into his pocket and pulled out a strip of jerky. Looking at the food, he realized he had no stomach for eating and threw it on the ground. It was a waste but seemed like the only thing to do—like some sort of primal, sacrificial offering to the mountain.

Jukka shook his head and began poking around in the gear for some kind of sign as to what had happened. A layer of the thick, black sludge that caked his boots quickly spread over his hands and forearms. One of his men had collected all the rifles and was bundling them up to be carried back. Another was now stacking the muddied packs together onto two large tree branches that they had collected just outside of the crater. They planned to construct a litter to drag as much of this down the mountain as they could. Eventually they would have to abandon the litter and distribute the supplies for each man to carry on his back down the remainder of the mountain.

As Jukka walked the site, one of his men ran up to him carrying a handful of bullet slugs. Each one was mushroomed out, and several were shattered. The magistrate and his hunting party had shot something, but the bullets had not penetrated whatever it was that they had hit. Jukka took one of the deformed lead slugs and turned it side to side in his fingers. Bullets typically shattered into fragments if they hit something like granite; the shape of this slug was strange. He tried to picture in his mind what could result in this interesting profile. It was as if the bullet had penetrated a softer material, slowing its velocity, and then struck something extremely hard. But in that scenario, the bullet would have remained trapped.

Jukka handed the slug back to the man and turned away, deep in thought.

Using his walking stick, he brushed through the piles of wet ash. He wasn't sure exactly what more he was searching for, trying absentmindedly to make sure they didn't miss an opportunity to locate any items that might be of sentimental value to the families back home or a further clue that would allow him to determine exactly what had taken place here. There was nothing worse to Jukka than this exact situation where loved ones were missing but no closure was possible. He hated the thought of a person left to suffer emotionally by hanging onto the thinnest thread of hope, when each passing day seems to confirm that such hope is futile.

After an hour or so, the team had recovered almost everything that had belonged to the hunting party, and they were all eager to head back toward Orneth and to get as far away from this disturbing site as possible.

Standing up, Jukka pushed over an upended ammo storage box to look inside before loading it onto one of the piles of the hunting party's belongings that waited to be returned to Orneth. Beneath the container, half buried in the mud and ash, was a small cloth bag with a piece of wet paper pinned to it. The ink was running but clearly read 'Isolde'.

Tears welled up in his eyes as he thought of Isolde, the magistrate's young wife, waiting back in Orneth, a new mother caring for their first child. Ghost letters bleeding through the damp paper told him there was more written inside. Jukka did not know what either the bag or letter contained within, nor did he have any intention of opening them to find out. He would take it to Isolde. If there was indeed anything inside that Isolde thought anyone else needed to know about, she would say so.

Jukka turned the bag over in his hands; whatever was inside was very heavy. He tucked it into his pocket without saying anything to anyone. He did not want people questioning Isolde about what her husband had left behind to her and their newborn son, or as to any last words he might have inscribed within. Jukka decided these things were no one else's business but Isolde's.

Looking around at this miserable scene, Jukka could not shake the feeling of how utterly strange it seemed. Something very bizarre and unnatural had happened here, and it just did not make sense. He knew all too well, though, that in times of crises and catastrophic events, any manner of strange things could happen; humans did odd and unpredictable things when they were frightened or scared.

He was trying to decide if there was anything more that his team could do here, when another man came nervously up to him carrying a long bundle of loosely wrapped burlap.

Jukka abandoned his thoughts of staying any longer when he pulled back the burlap to see what the man held. A fetid odor preceded whatever was hidden by the cloth; this was a scent that Jukka had encountered many times over his years spent in the outdoors, and what followed that stench was generally not a pleasant sight—this was the smell of death. While he accepted death as a normal mechanism of life, it was not something he wanted on the forefront of his mind while out searching for his lost friends and fellow citizens.

Both Jukka and the man holding the fabric contorted their faces in response to the smell, and gasped. Bile rose in his throat, accompanied by a distinct dull pain in his gut, as Jukka contemplated what horrific evidence of what had happened here might be contained within.

Inside the cloth was about the last thing Jukka expected to see at over three thousand meters above sea level. Mottled red and gray, over six inches in diameter and longer than Jukka's arm, was a section of a tentacle from what was clearly a giant squid.

CHAPTER TWO
(A Keepsake Shared)

"Pax, I need to give you something," said Isolde, Pax's mother. She took him firmly by the shoulders and spoke softly but seriously. She stared deeply into his anxious, hazel eyes.

"You need to keep this and protect this," she continued. "At some point, someone from a long time away will try to take this from you – they must not succeed. You need to be prepared to do whatever is necessary to guard this."

Isolde was very petite and looked far younger than her age. Her chestnut hair was pulled back into a short ponytail, and the color was accented pleasantly by her saffron yellow robe. She knelt down onto the floor and indicated for her son to do the same. Pax looked down at the wide, walnut planks. He loved the warmth of the various hand-polished woods in their home, especially when the firelight flickered through the steel grate of the stove door and ignited the detail of the grain.

The room in which they sat was very simple but steeped in dignity and thoughtful design. The dark walnut floor spread out across the room and butted into the large marble blocks that formed the walls. Each chunk of the marble was nearly pure white, and although not identical in size, each block was far heavier than one man could move alone. The craftsmanship involved in placing such stones of disparate size to create a wall of uniform dimension was impressive, as was the effort put into each and every element comprising their home.

Enormous beams of hickory ran overhead, supporting the thick slate panels that formed the roof. Pax often reclined on the floor by the stove to enjoy the heat of the fire, and to watch the shadows shape-shift across the ceiling above. He gazed for hours at the range of colors interspersed throughout the slate, from thick honey-yellows to blood-orange reds, from algae blue-greens to the countless chalky, earthen grays. On rainy days, he searched for creatures and mythological heroes hidden within the subtle variations of the slate, just as he did with the clouds outside on sunny days. Pax in no way suffered from a lack of imagination and this ceiling had always been a comfortable sounding board for his thoughts and ideas.

The black cast iron stove stood in the corner, flanked by a moderate supply of firewood Pax had split earlier in the week. A deep orange glow radiated outward, accompanied by the comforting crackle of the burning wood. Thick rugs, made from the wool of their own sheep, sprawled out in several areas around the room, the soft loose curls of the fringe spreading lazily out onto the walnut. Intricate patterns, abundant in deep, rich colors, were woven into the fabrics. Sitting upon a deep-crimson carpet graced with a sun motif radiating from the center, Isolde reached into the folds of her robe and removed something Pax could not distinguish.

Pax's mother handed him a small linen bag. He studied the rough ecru fabric. The henna stains and threadbare spots from years of handling spoke of the obvious age of the bag, and of the contents as well, Pax guessed. Dark stains spread upward from the bottom of the bag, as if it had sat in mud at some point in time.

He gently took the bag from his mother and noticed that its weight was much greater than he had expected for something so small. The knot in the frayed cord that held it closed opened easily, and a heavy pocket watch slid out.

A sense of power and as yet undefined purpose flowed through Pax as he held the object. He visibly shuddered and glanced up at his mother; strangely, she did not seem at all startled by this reaction. Pax felt the sensation of energy emanate from this item and wondered if this timepiece was powered by some internal electrical source. At the same time he sensed this energy, his mind seemed to open and expand, and he knew these impressions were related and inseparable. Holding this article somehow filled a small part of the hole lingering in Pax's heart — the emptiness of never knowing his father. Suddenly, that hole seemed smaller, and he miraculously felt a connection to his father through this watch.

"Your father left that for us," Isolde said solemnly.

Pax nodded in agreement. He had already sensed that before Isolde spoke the words.

Although his soul felt lighter, Pax was again struck by the weight of the watch; it did not seem possible for something of this size to have so much mass. He knew gold was heavy, but even if this thing had been solid, he would not have guessed it could weigh so much. The piece was ornate and beautiful. At first glance, the myriad of symbols and designs graced the cover in a haphazard way. Looking closely at the details of the watch's cover and of the visible perimeter of the case, Pax began to sense a purpose to the design. A vignette of an open plain graced the cover; the hemisphere of the sun shone over the horizon that bisected the cover of the timepiece. Pax presupposed the sun in the image was rising, not setting. He could not explain this feeling, but had grown to trust his intuition over his relatively short life. A large hourglass occupied the center of the scene, and he presumed that the artisan's intent was for the hourglass to appear close to the viewer, not as a huge hourglass sitting inexplicably in the middle of an expansive plain.

Something seemed incongruous in the scene that he had not been able to identify, but after a few moments, he realized what was wrong: the hourglass was upside down. The sand was flowing from the bottom lobe up into the upper and finally settling on the top of the hourglass.

Time flowing backward, drifted across Pax's thoughts.

Beautiful gold filigree of amazingly fine detail gracefully and subtly filled in various open spaces within the vignette, hinting to Pax of invisible things such as wind and warmth. A serpentine band of thorned vines encircled the top portion of the visible case. Exactly half of the vine curving from the crown at the top, down the right side, all the way to the hinge at the bottom, was thick with leaves and loaded with full, ripe fruits of all varieties. From the hinge, moving upwards toward the crown to the left side, the vine was barren and devoid of leaves, bristling with long, sharp thorns. As Pax followed the carving from the crown downward to the right, he had the sense of walking through a calm meadow permeated with peace and prosperity. As he continued on past the hinge and along the vine with no leaves or fruit, he felt alone and isolated, as if moving into a wasteland of oblivion and despair.

The word *mandala* passed through Pax's consciousness as he considered all of the elements on the cover as one symbol. He was vaguely familiar with the idea of the word but could not specifically recall the definition.

Moving downward from the point where the horizon line moved off of the watch face to the right were five phases of the moon, starting at full, quarter, half, three-quarter, and back to full at the bottom above the hinge. Two symbols, an alpha and an omega, along with a pyramid, floated above the phases of the moon. Curving around the edge of the bottom left quadrant were five raised stars. The bottom star had eight points, each one diminishing by one point until the fifth star just below the horizon, which had four points. Each star was linked to the center of the horizon by a series of dotted lines. Spanning the sky were six irregularly spaced rays of light, each tipped with a small triangle, originating from behind the profile of a mountain range. As he traced the jagged profile of the peaks, he gasped.

This is was Zeitlos-Granit!

Pax's mind raced as he thought of the implications. *Had the watch been made here in Orneth?* Pax did not believe watches had ever been made in Orneth.

Watches in general were uncommon, and at the ripe old age of thirteen, Pax had not yet owned one. Even so, he instinctively depressed the crown, releasing the lid, which gently sprung open.

Pax heard Isolde catch her breath. "Be careful," she whispered.

He opened the lid and looked at the face, where he was immediately struck by the complete absence of any indicators of time. A single red hand that curved in a sweeping S slashed from the center downward toward what would traditionally have been between five and six o'clock.

This is not a watch at all, Pax thought, and then said the same aloud.

Pax lifted his gaze to meet his mother's dark eyes, and was struck by the sense of fear and helplessness he saw within (which is eye-opening for a child to see in the countenance of a parent—the first step towards true realization that parents are actually *human*). Typically Isolde was brimming with life and full of warmth. Tonight, not even the glow and heat that radiated from the fire and danced softly across her face could warm her eyes or melt the chill of melancholy present there.

Her expression made it clear that she did not know what this golden object was or its purpose, but Pax had no doubt that she somehow thought that all of these things would be made clear by him. This embattled uncertainty and hope that showed in his mother's face placed a sense of responsibility upon his shoulders that felt like the weight of the world—at the very least, the weight of their small world.

Pax had never known his father. His mother told him wonderful stories of the man. He was strong and intelligent, but quiet. Although not particularly interested in politics, he was a natural leader. The people of Orneth had continually looked to him for sound advice and come to rely on his fair-minded decisions. Avoiding this mantle as long as he could, he had eventually relented and agreed to be magistrate of Orneth.

This had occurred during the time that Isolde was pregnant with Pax, their first son. She had smiled watching her husband concede to the wishes of the people, certain he was the best man for the job. Isolde was filled with pride for her husband, knowing full well he had accepted such a responsibility solely to make Orneth the best place possible to raise and nurture their forthcoming child.

According to Isolde, it was less than a year after Pax had been born that his father and a group of other men had gone into the mountains on an annual hunting expedition.

The second night of their journey, when they were already well up into the recesses of the Zeitlos-Granit, a severe weather front rolled in from the south, quite unexpected for this time of the year. From Orneth, the townspeople stood outside in the torrential rain and blustering wind, fascinated by the intensity of the electrical storm over the mountain range. Violet flashes of lightning hammered away at the mountain range as if punishing it for some unknown transgression.

No one returned. After waiting for nearly two weeks, search parties finally went out looking, but did not find even a single trace of the group.

Over the years, Pax had heard similar stories of groups of men disappearing without a trace under bizarre circumstances. Isolde would never talk in more detail, no matter how many questions Pax asked. Eventually he stopped pressing her, thinking she would talk about what had happened when and if she was ready.

"You remember Jukka Hendrikkson, he led one of the search parties that went out looking for your father," Isolde said, interrupting his thoughts in such a way that it seemed she could tell exactly what he was thinking. "Jukka was the best climber in Orneth, and he took his search team farther up into the Zeitlos than anyone thought your father's hunting party could have reached. Jukka himself was probably the only person who had ever climbed into some of those far recesses.

"Jukka found an area where your father and his men had stood and fought against someone or something, he thought perhaps a group of bandits or a pack of wolves. There was a makeshift redoubt, and the ground was covered with spent shell casings." Isolde looked off into the distance.

Although they sat within the shelter of their home, Pax knew Isolde was looking far beyond the walls and up into the heartless peaks of the Zeitlos-Granit. What his mother had just shared was far more information than she had ever related to him before

"But why has everyone always said no one found a trace?" Pax asked.

"Jukka felt there was something very bizarre and mysterious about the scene they had discovered. He felt that this would only create more questions than it answered for the families who had potentially lost loved ones. While I didn't agree with this way of dealing with this, Jukka argued that there was still a glimmer of hope and that he wanted to keep that hope alive. He had a big heart and did not want anyone to suffer the pain of such a loss."

Isolde continued, "I think much of this was because his wife had disappeared in an avalanche a few years prior, and he was convinced that one day she would return." Isolde shifted her position slightly for comfort.

"The search parties that had looked for his wife had never found her or her climbing party. In Jukka's mind, the absence of definitive proof that she had died, meant that there was hope, and he felt he should continue searching.

"It was the same way with the scene they had stumbled upon while looking for your father; while it had been bizarre and disturbing, no actual evidence was found that your father and his hunting party had perished. Jukka took that to mean they could still be alive.

"If Jukka told everyone in Orneth of the strange scene, then everyone would have assumed something terrible had happened to them. He convinced his men to hide what they had found in the mountains and to keep this secret to themselves as a way to give hope to the families and prevent the lives of these respected men from being remembered only by the mystery of their disappearance.

"I saw Jukka years back, preparing to head up into the mountains once again. He told me that he just needed to hike for a few days to get some exercise, but I knew that he continued to search for all those lost and unaccounted for.

"Jukka never returned - you were probably too young to recall the memorial service held for him in the village."

"That's sad. It seems that disaster followed anyone with any association to my father's hunting trip." Pax commented. "But there must have been more at the site where he found this," he held up the watch, "to make the scene seem so strange," Pax concluded.

He's very perceptive, thought Isolde. *He knows I'm withholding some details.*

"You're right, Pax. What was really the most bizarre thing was that Jukka found a section of what he thought was a giant squid's tentacle. It was cleanly severed at one end and riddled with bullet wounds from the types of rifles your father's hunting party carried."

"That is very odd," Pax said. His brow furrowed as it always did when he contemplated difficult or challenging problems. The presence of a giant squid high up in the Zeitlos-Granit defied logic; Pax did not even know where to begin speculating as to how such a discovery could be possible. The people of Orneth were not fishermen, so it did not make sense that someone would have carried this for food. And if for some strange reason they had, it made even less sense it would be filled with bullets.

Tucking this thought away to ponder later, he moved on.

"So Jukka told you all of these things that have been held secret all these years; how did you get this?" Pax asked respectfully, firelight glinting on the golden object he held up.

"Good question, Pax," his mother replied. "Jukka was the last to leave the scene after deciding it was time to return to Orneth. On his last sweep of the area, he found that bag with a handwritten note to me attached," Isolde replied. "That was inside."

He looked closely at the inside the shiny cover.

"Tempus fugit in totus advectum

To places far and near

Though through the glass dimly now,

All things will soon be clear"

read the inscription on the inside of the shiny gold cover.

"Time flies in all places?" Pax translated aloud. "I think I understand the individual words, but this phrase doesn't make any sense to me."

The smoothness of the gold allowed Pax to clearly see his reflection around the beautiful script of the strange words, partially written in the ancient, dead language. Pax had always loved Latin and yearned for the return of its common use.

"All things will become clear over time," Isolde said. She spoke in a tone that sounded as if she was reading someone else's words. "That's what your father's note said. That part was for you Pax, not me." A chill ran up her spine as she realized the similarity of the words from her husband's note and those Pax had just read from the inside the golden cover.

Isolde explained that the note had been hurriedly written, obviously under duress, so this phrase must carry real importance. One other point that was clear was a statement to the reader 'not to adjust the device until its function was completely understood'. She had taken the warning seriously, and as a result had never opened the lid of the object.

"When Jukka gave this to me, he shared everything I've just told you. He begged me to keep his secret for just a few more weeks while he continued to search. A few weeks turned into a few months, and then into a few years. After that… well, life just went on. Everyone just began to assume that the men had died in the storm. Mystery or not, that may be what happened after all. In any case, your father never returned."

Questions flooded though his mind, but he did not want to burden his mother further by asking for more information that she either did not know, or did not want to share. Instead, he hugged her tightly and told her not to worry. Such were the exact things his mother needed; such was the behavior that told her that her boy, tempered by the mantle of responsibility and the weight of what seemed nothing short of a supernatural destiny, had become a man. He had emerged from an emotional trial by fire without visible consequence, but Isolde was certain that Pax would be called to stand a much more severe test at some point in his life. She felt that he would do well, but was not so certain about her ability to be a witness to such events.

Isolde looked weary. Pax suggested that she go to bed and let her know he would go out for a walk under the stars. She hugged him again and looked at him as only a mother can look at a son who is maturing before her eyes. Torn by the sadness of her baby's departure, she felt the pride of success in watching the young man she had raised arrive to take his place.

Pax was already tall, taking after his father's family. His hair was chestnut like hers, but longer and thicker. Isolde saw the muscles in his chest, arms, and legs, and knew he was filling out into his already broad shoulders. The mysterious golden device had looked like a toy in his hands as compared to hers.

His hazel eyes were flecked with gold and were striking, although Pax blushed with embarrassment when Isolde described them so. Pax could convey the qualities of strength, confidence, and kindness, with just a simple glance. Those close to him also sometimes saw a distant loneliness.

All mothers think their sons handsome, but Isolde had noticed for some time now the way the young women and older girls now looked at Pax when he was working or walking through the village, and could tell by their lingering glances and coquettish smiles that they shared her opinion.

Walking beneath the canopy of bright stars that saturated the inky blackness above, Pax's emotions were torn; one minute his heart was heavy from the fresh memories and talk concerning the loss of his father. In the next moment, he was elated by the sense of purpose and excitement carried in his mother's words and from the energy that seemed to radiate from the gold object weighing around his neck. As Pax scanned the night skies, comforted by the familiar formations of stars, he saw a new constellation in the eastern sky, that of a beautiful lotus flower filling the hemisphere. He was awestruck by the brightness and clarity, the beautiful symmetry and unmistakable image. Despite the coolness of the night, Pax stretched out in the deep grass and stared up at this newly formed stellar design.

He went to sleep that night thinking of what his mother had said. Normally his mother was clear, concise, and eloquent, which was why he was so puzzled over her use of the phrase "someone will come *from a long time away* and try to take this from you."

Pax thought he should ask her about her semantics; was that phrase from his father's note?

"A long time away," he whispered as he drifted into sleep. He dreamt that night of a lotus flower among the stars. He awoke refreshed in the soft purple light of the early morning with a sense of purpose and a vision for the future. He knew he would assemble his closest friends to help him in his task of protecting the strange device, and that he would call this collective the Order of the Celestial Lotus.

Although he scanned the skies intently each night after, Pax never saw the lotus constellation again, and he never shared this story with anyone.

As with many ideas that come with the cover of night, the thought of asking his mother about her enigmatic words faded with the morning light. So Pax never inquired about her strange reference to someone coming from a long time away. He was brimming with excitement about putting together the Order of the Celestial Lotus. Pax already had his close circle of friends who formed an inseparable band; he just needed to tell them the story. It never crossed his mind that any of these friends would object. None did.

The Order of the Celestial Lotus consisted of Pax, Veronica, Isaiah-Jung, Sören, Eckhardt, Agathi, and Sasha. Lifelong friends all, they had been around each other since they were babies and had gone through all of the trials of maturing into teenagers. Technically, Pax and Veronica had known each other the longest since their parents had been next-door neighbors; they had always been especially close. While their mothers both secretly hoped (and everyone else assumed) that this pair would someday marry, Pax and Veronica had never been aware of this secret, unspoken assumption, and had shown no proclivity to complying with Destiny on this particular point.

This team trained together in physical combat as a group, and each pursued individual interests that always seemed to benefit the group collectively. Years passed, and really good friends became enduring best friends.

Every member of the Order had been born in Orneth with the exception of Agathi, who had been adopted from an orphanage as an infant and grown up here. Agathi had been given the name Helen at the orphanage and her parents simply added Agathi. There was no orphanage in Orneth, and when she had arrived there was apparently some air of mystery surrounding her appearance from some faraway place. Pax recalled as a very young boy hearing some of the older women whisper about this, and heard words such as *cloister* and *convent*. He had heard Agathi referred to more than once as Helen of the Rock.

None of these memories carried any mystery for Pax or any other member of the Order of the Celestial Lotus; to them, Agathi was Agathi, whom they all loved dearly. None of them remembered any events surrounding their own birth either and no one particularly cared.

Families tended to remain in the same village, rarely leaving the village proper, much less leaving the family home in which they were born. As a result, the houses were collections of small additions, each of which could typically be used to count the number of generations living within. Their village, Orneth, was nestled in the rolling green steppes near the rocky mountain range, the Zeitlos-Granit. Beyond the Zeitlos-Granit, the terrain gradually became more arid, and desert sands completely consumed the landscape within a few weeks' walk. But that was another world altogether that held no lure for Pax at this point in time; there was plenty of adventure right here in his very own.

Buildings here in Orneth were mostly single-story structures that merged into the hills and conformed to the horizon from almost every angle, each constructed primarily of the natural materials found in the area: rusty granite, chalky white limestone, and iron. Also used were the remnants excavated from the ruins of the Ecology War between the Unified States and the Developing States. Relations between these two predominant world powers had deteriorated and eventually led to a global nuclear war. The post-war world was an interesting mixture of modern and primitive, as was reflected in villages like Orneth—a world that had computers and oxcarts, advanced education in an agrarian society, and no real major cities. The metropolises had been the primary targets during the first nuclear military exchanges in the Ecology War, and as a result, they had been the most decimated. History recorded that these ruined structures had been buried with earth to try and protect them from the radiation that saturated them. The danger had long since faded, and the material from which the sprawling cities had been constructed was safe to use now. Subsequently, many homes had walls of thick plate glass and beams of titanium integrated into their design, elements that were common in the design of buildings at the time of the Ecology Wars. Electricity was not produced in any one central location, nor was there any centralized grid designed to distribute electricity through the village. Hospitals and other critical facilities had their own moderate generators, and there were small generators located at sporadic substations around the village that were accessible to the general public.

Another interesting by-product of society's separation from such a dependence upon technology was the revival of oral histories. In using the spoken word, it was an accepted tradition that such discourses be shared in their original language, leading to a focus on multi-lingual fluency.

Pax loved Orneth and had never been plagued by the desire to leave that many youth felt around his age. He felt blessed to have a loving mother, a beautiful home, and close friends. Pax often thought that no one could have asked for a better group of friends with which to battle some yet-unrevealed enemy, much less to stand by his side while going through all the wonderful adventures in everyday life.

CHAPTER THREE
(Two Strangers)

Veronica focused intently on the target situated over fifty meters away. Her voluminous henna-colored mane was pulled up into two flowing pigtails that sprouted upwards and then swept down well past her waist. Despite her best effort, wisps of her beautiful locks had escaped, and the gentle breeze moved them across her field of vision. But it took more than strands of hair to deter Veronica's focus, and she had her sights set on a bull's-eye. She held the bowstring firmly pulled taut and lightly against her cheek, moving the point of the hammered iron arrowhead minutely to the right to compensate for the wind. Her large eyes were intent, and the sun illuminated the deep purple of her irises, creating a starburst of varying shades of violet.

Veronica was tall and muscular but remained thin. A year ago, she would have been described as gangly, but she had outgrown that phase and had developed into a beautiful young woman. The first thing people generally noticed about Veronica was her hair. The color was a pleasing henna, but not in and of itself cause for a second glance; it was the sheer *volume* of her hair that captured peoples' attention.

When straightened, it fell down past her knees and was so full and thick that it probably weighed as much as the rest of her, more when wet.

Even when the air was still, Veronica's hair seemed to constantly swirl and snake about, giving her the appearance of an angelic Medusa— except that catching sight of her tended to warm peoples' hearts instead of turning them to stone. Her locks seemed to take on a life of their own and rarely cooperated with what Veronica had in mind, but nevertheless always appeared striking.

She loosed the arrow and followed its invisible course as it covered the distance to find its mark in the yellow center of the target.

My aim is true, thought Veronica.

"Nice shot!" Isaiah-Jung yelled as he looked up from sharpening a large pike in time to see the arrow strike the target dead center. He was kneeling in the thick green grass, with the blade of the pike resting against a large section of a felled hickory tree, cracked and split with age. They always spoke of this as "the tree that had been struck by lightning." (None of them had witnessed this, of course; the tree had in fact been stretched out here as long as any of them could remember. But this was nevertheless what this piece of wood was called.) The entire group had hiked out to this large clearing, one of their favorite spots to spend a day together when they had no other responsibilities.

Veronica beamed and curtsied in Isaiah-Jung's direction. A pink flush spread across her already rosy cheeks.

"I'll give you my share of lunch if you can do that again!" Sören called out from a shady spot where he sat reading with Agathi. Sasha was close by, adding wood to the fire and generally busy preparing lunch.

Veronica moved with a fluid grace and was very strong despite her lithe physique. She was renowned for her ability to eat, and eat, and eat.

"You're on!" Veronica called back. She pulled an arrow with beautiful feather fletching from the sheath that hung from her belt. She had made this arrow herself using brass to fashion an ornately designed head, a shaft that blended mahogany and ash, and the feathers of a rare albatross for the fletching.

Veronica's determination was set in the tense lines of her face as she once again squared off at the target. Her concentration returned, and the surroundings faded away.

Sören, Isaiah-Jung, Sasha, and Agathi all stopped their activities to watch the challenge. Eckhardt emerged from a small tent wearing some strange goggles that made him look like a mutated insect. Eckhardt was shorter than the other young men. He was thinner, but not skinny, with broad shoulders and muscular arms. Eckhardt had sandy blonde hair and kept it short on the back and sides, but somehow ended up with a huge mound of flowing hair piled up on the top of his head. This mass inevitably fell across his face and blocked his eyes or shot off in some wayward direction.

One lens of the goggles he wore looked like a telescoping binocular lens turned backward, where Eckhardt was looking in the large end out through the small. He rotated a ring at the base of this lens that protruded several inches out, and Pax could see the telescoping sections move in and out accordingly. The other lens consisted of short, squat cylinder that had the same diameter its entire length. A slight green glow seemed to emanate from the convex lens at the end of this cylinder, and a rainbow of color danced across the surface of the glass when it faced the sunlight.

Eckhardt was the scientist of the group and spent all of his spare time developing some innovative gadget. The entire group was very well-learned, but often when Eckhardt attempted to describe one of his projects, the details went far over their heads, especially when it related to electronics or optics, such as this current invention.

Turning the diopter at the end of the shorter lens allowed him to focus in Veronica's direction. Eckhardt's view of the scene was very different than what the others saw in the bright morning sunlight. In the glowing lens, Veronica was clearly visible on the horizon, but she was a mass of various colors. In the center of her profile was red. Then she was yellow, orange, green, and finally outlined in radiant purple. The beautiful blue sky and green grass all appeared completely black.

When he closed this eye and looked at her through the telescoping lens, the background was a dull green with Veronica displayed as a wireframe figure; various numbers and measurements glowed at specific points around the image, each changing as he moved his head. He flipped a lever on the side of the lens and a slightly magnified view of his normal vision appeared.

Veronica stood statuesque on the horizon, the archetypal profile of Diana the Archer. Just as she prepared to loose the arrow, a familiar voice rang out, taking everyone aback and breaking Veronica's focus on the target. Fortunately, she didn't let her prized arrow fly off haphazardly.

Sören's challenge for lunch would have to wait.

Pax marched over the hill with an elderly gentleman wearing an earthen green robe in tow close behind.

"Hello, everyone!" Pax called out again. "Please join me.

"This is Dhaal. He has told me that he has knowledge of our mission, of our task to protect the artifact. He feels that it is important for us to be aware."

"Where did you find him?" asked Sören. He placed a bookmark into the tome that he carried while walking toward Pax and their guest. He stopped and looked up as he closed the book.

"Sören! Please show appropriate respect," Pax chided.

Dhaal stepped into the circle and into the conversation. "Don't worry Pax," he started, "Sören has always been cautious of strangers, which is not a bad quality in these questionable times."

Sören was taken aback at such an observation by a man he had never met.

Does this man know me? Sören thought. *Perhaps he knows my grandparents and they have told him about me.*

While caught off-guard and feeling at a disadvantage, he was at the same time captivated by Dhaal's soothing voice and the sense of presence. The gentleman seemed larger than life as Sören now took the time to observe him; one could not help but to take note of the strength that flowed out from him. He was slightly taller than those who stood in the circle, with the exception of Isaiah-Jung. His hair was pure white and pulled up into a plait in the very center of his scalp, held tightly there by a brass cylinder.

The elder man's skin was weathered and spotted from age, like many older men who spent a great amount of time outdoors. His arms and legs were thick and sinewy; Dhaal had been no stranger to hard physical work. Dhaal's robe was of a heavy fabric unfamiliar to Sören and was dyed with a deep emerald green color that Sören had never seen before in a fabric. Dhaal's long robes were gathered up and secured around his thighs in a swath, revealing dusty feet protected by sandals that were equally worn and weathered. A thickening waistline indicated that Dhaal had a healthy appetite and that he had access to an abundance of food.

Sören returned to the stranger's comment; the fact remained that Sören *had* always been cautious of strangers and tended to talk of them in the third person, even in their presence.

This personality trait was sometimes perceived as rudeness and had been a foible of his as long as he could recall. His grandparents had raised him and had probably been the ones to instill this caution in him.

"My apologies, Dhaal," Sören started, "I *am* cautious of those I do not know. No disrespect intended."

"None taken."

"Dhaal sought me out as the result of a dream he had," Pax continued. "He says that Kismet brought us together just in time."

"Just in time for what?" Isaiah-Jung queried.

"In time for what you've waited for all these years, for what you've known would come. I'm saying nothing new when I emphasize that you must protect that which you've been entrusted to protect." The old man's piercing hazel eyes calmly scanned the circle, looking deeply into each one's face.

Veronica sheathed her special arrow, glad she had saved it, fixated by their visitor.

Dhaal continued, "He comes to claim that which Pax protects, that which *he* believes is *his*."

"Who is this mystery person that we've waited for all this time?" Sasha asked. "It would be nice to put a name to the one we've guarded against all these years."

"This I do not know, but I have a sense that you should be prepared to deal with more than one aggressor, but I cannot clarify what that might mean. There is definitely one leader, but I do feel that he is surrounded by many minions. In any case, I believe all of these questions will be answered soon. Very soon." Dhaal made a sweeping gesture and stood with his palms stretched outward at his waist.

"How do you know all this?" Eckhardt chimed in. "How will we know when this time comes?"

"You ask many of the same questions I have asked myself," the elderly man responded. "As I said, much of this is an intuitive feeling that has come to me in dreams. Early on, I saw Pax clearly and knew that he protected something from a malevolent force that was seeking him out."

"It is difficult to describe, but I infer most of the meaning of my visions based on how they color my mood.

"Again, I saw Pax, but did not see him in any context that would indicate where he was. Several times, I have seen your village clearly, sitting against this profile of the Zeitlos."

When Dhaal said the words "sitting against this profile," he held up his hands and moved them to frame the village in the distance.

"I have many dreams and visions, as do we all. This place, as well as many of you, has appeared in these dreams. The mountain was very clear, as was Pax, but some of your characteristics were clearer than your faces. Sören was there, for example, and there was always a young woman with unique hair." Dhaal nodded toward Veronica. "But never so beautiful in my dreams as in reality."

Veronica blushed.

"I was not traveling in pursuit of those in this vision, but I always remain open to the reality contained within my dreams. I did not know specifically where this village was, but the landscape began to seem very familiar as I traveled, and I have never passed though this area. This prompted me to describe the village in my vision and sketch out the profile of this part of the mountain range to someone in a village about two days' walk from here, and he directed me to Orneth. This detour puts me about four days off of my schedule. But as the elements in my dreams became more real, so did the sense of urgency that I find you."

"Surely you can stay with us at least for the day?" Agathi said. She had quickly developed an opinion of Dhaal, and it was obviously a good one.

"I cannot stay at this time. There are things I must tend to; I must continue on," Dhaal explained. "But I do feel such a great sense of relief at being able to pass on this torch of worry that I've carried, the feeling that I needed to find Pax and share this however irrelevant vision with him. I have lightened the burden of my soul. I'm glad I met Pax and had the chance to warn you that your enemy approaches very soon."

"Dhaal will cross into the lands where the Suleiman once ruled and then trek up to north, to where the Cyrills live, where the sun stays up for months at a time," Pax informed the group. "Sasha, I believe your distant relatives come from that region."

Sasha nodded in agreement.

"Have you been south of the Zeitlos, Dhaal?" Agathi asked seriously, pointing off into the distance.

Dhaal lowered his gaze.

"Yes, Agathi. I visited there with my father when I was much younger than you, I would guess. So ..."

"I've heard that people practice magic there," Agathi said. Coming from any of those standing in this group, a statement like this would have drawn laughter. But looking at the seriousness visible on Agathi's face, no one even smirked. In fact, everyone turned to Dhaal, awaiting his response.

"There are many strange and mysterious things there that I would prefer not to discuss. Besides, I was young, and memories can get confused with stories and legends as the years pass. Many things that seemed scary when I was a child now seem benign when I think back upon them. Anyway, I have had neither the inclination nor opportunity to return."

Dhaal turned and looked toward the mountain range in silence, shuffling through his memories from many years before.

"Are you sure you can't stay with us?" Dhaal was clearly finished with this topic, and Sasha asked the question, anxious to change the subject. "Lunch is almost ready. At least stay and eat with us."

"Thank you for your kind offer, but alas, I cannot. As Pax said, the sun stays up for months at a time where I am headed, but later in the season, it also doesn't rise for months at a time, either. I'd like to arrive when the sun remains up in the sky." Dhaal smiled. His eyes glittered. He had said that he was relieved, but he still looked saddled with responsibility.

"As you can see," Dhaal said, patting his belly, "I am not in danger of starving!"

Dhaal clasped each one's hand and wished them all the best. He told them that no matter what they encountered, that they should remain true to themselves and that they should be comforted by the knowledge that they were standing for what is true and right.

"So many times in life, the choices you face are rarely so clear, rarely so Aristotelian," Dhaal said as he turned to go. "Find peace in the clarity of facing a challenge in such obvious terms of white and black, of good and evil."

Dhaal moved westward as the morning sun moved higher in the rich ultramarine sky. He raised a hand and waved to the group without looking back.

The smells of lentil soup and roast pheasant filled the air. Everyone knew that Sasha had made fresh tortillas earlier that morning and that she would brew mint tea as well. Everyone was hungry, especially Veronica.

They sat and ate the wonderful food that Sasha had prepared, and generally enjoyed the beauty of the day. Everyone helped clean up and congregated around the tree that had been struck by lightning to enjoy more tea, to sit and read, or just to watch the several hawks drifting above, carried by the gentle breeze.

"I like Dhaal," said Agathi as she rested against the tree, staring up into the sky. "I wish he could stay with us for a while. We could use him in the OCL."

"The Order of the Celestial Lotus is fine," Sören said.

"He did seem nice," Isaiah-Jung said, "but I'm not sure he really told us anything we didn't know."

"Just that the one we're waiting for will come soon," said Sasha.

"That's somewhat like the guy who is always chanting that the end of the world is near. Every day that is truer than the day before, and eventually he'll be right. But it's not specific enough to help," Sören commented.

"That's all true," Pax said, kneeling down and brushing his hand through the grass, "but I have a feeling that it was important Dhaal came into our lives."

Veronica undid the leather quiver from her waist. Pax had made the quiver for her years ago. It was made from leather that he had tanned and dyed. Beautiful carvings of the hills that surrounded Orneth encircled the quiver, with the Zeitlos-Granit centered on one side. Veronica thought it funny how the image of this same mountain had influenced Dhaal, a stranger from far away. She added, "He said things will be clearer soon. How will we know?"

"We will know," Sören said. "Look!"

The group followed Sören's arm pointing up to the westward sky. Their gaze saw a maelstrom of dark clouds beginning to spiral outward from a single point within the clear sky. The fabric of the sky itself seemed to ripple, like the shockwave created by a stone plunging into a still pond.

A burst of bright violet light erupted from the eye of the spinning mass. The light was accompanied by a thunderous wall of sound, the energy of which drove the few of the group that were now standing backward. Everyone was confused, stunned, and slightly blinded by the light.

As the group regained their sight and footing, they were stunned by the sight of a hideous apparition floating in their midst.

Three times the height of an average man, this creature was a mix of organic and mechanical elements, and by far the strangest thing anyone standing there had ever seen. The core of the thing before them was a large, clear, ovoid body, outwardly supported by a metallic structure from which two arms radiated; both mechanical and human components were visibly interwoven.

Static discharges exploded randomly from all around the metal exoskeleton and then dissipated.

Pax watched the hands; they had the appearance of being large male hands with thick fingers and the heavy swollen knuckles of a sixty-year-old human that had not been a stranger to physical labor.

The right forearm that supported the hand upon which he focused consisted of a large clear tube full of a translucent green liquid. Spanning the entire length of this clear tube were large muscles, devoid of skin and human in appearance. The ligaments originated at a large hinged elbow and disappeared into a cap that sealed one end of the tube; this housed a metallic ball and socket assembly on which the hand seemed to rotate.

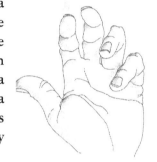

A writhing mass of tentacles carried the bizarre amalgam of elements that made up the main torso of this being. These snakelike arms were long and thin like that of a giant squid, but there were far more than ten. Primarily a mottled red and gray, the underside of the arms, from which large suction cups protruded, were white. Some of the arms worked in unison to support the glass and metal torso that wavered above, while many just whipped about through the air or writhed along the ground, like antennae collecting information on the environment and relaying it back to their host.

But the most unique and captivating feature of this being were the eyes.

Centered in the clear egg-shaped dome was a spinning pyramid. On each of the four faces of the pyramid, a large eye stared outward. Far too large to be human eyes, but with human proportion, they cast an eerie and disturbing presence. The rate at which the pyramid spun seemed to change. Rotating slowly at first, it accelerated to a rate that was impossible to see, appearing only as a pyramidal blur. Finally, the pyramid seemed to stabilize at a fixed rate.

This process reminded Pax of a strobe that Eckhardt had shown him some time back; there was a thick spinning platter displaying a series of what appeared to Pax to be random black marks all around the edge. Eckhardt placed a small green light source pointing at the marked edge and turned a dial. The disk had started to spin and the marks became a blur. Turning the dial adjusted the speed at which the platter spun. By varying that rate, Eckhardt could make different bands of the marks appear as if they were moving forward, backward, or even standing completely still.

The effect of the pyramid's current rate of spin was haunting. The four large eyes seemed to merge into a single all-seeing eye that appeared to watch them from all points. Pax moved slowly to his left and then back to his right. The eye stared directly at him, no matter where he moved. He knew from his experience with Eckhardt's spinning platter that the eye would appear to follow him, even if he moved around this creature in a complete circle. He also knew that the illusion was the same for everyone, no matter where they stood. Pax had no intention of confirming this theory by starting to move around and draw any unnecessary attention now.

Pax had always been very keen at gauging a person's character by peering into his eyes, a true believer in the age-old adage that the eyes are the windows to the soul.

This eye was a window to a soul that could not exist.

Pax shuddered.

"I am Möbius! I travel the time-space continuum!"

the strange presence bellowed, shocking everyone from their individual speculation about this surreal sight.

"I have traveled to the edge of the universe and beyond into The Void itself! I am an artifact of creation, the one that sees all, past, present, and future! I bridge the beginning and the end. I am eternal!"

The words were loud and very clear, although Pax could not see the source of the voice. Rich in a baritone timbre, the voice had a paternal tone, full and firm. Spoken as if the name Möbius should be recognized, Pax vaguely recognized the word from either math or physics but he could not really recall now.

"I have come for what is mine!" the voice echoed. The hint of the paternal, if it had been present at all moments ago, had quickly been replaced by a mix of anger and desperation. Pax felt the words; the sounds seemed to register directly within his nervous system and not through his ears

"I have come for the Artifex Temporis."

"The what?" Pax asked, surprised that he had spoken at all. Pax understood the direct Latin translation but was unfamiliar with those words in this context. Regardless, he knew full well what the creature wanted. This was the enemy of which they had been forewarned and for which Dhaal had been a recent harbinger.

"Silence! You have anticipated my coming, and you have what it is that I seek."

"The watch?" Pax once again asked a rhetorical question.

"The Artifex Temporis!"

Möbius spoke the name again with a tone of respect and awe, with an undertone of disgust.

"I keep it hidden," Pax explained. "I don't carry it with me." He was in fact testing this apparition to see if he could tell that the watch weighed heavily on a chain around his neck. "It is two days journey from here."

"Return here in seven days. I will be waiting to claim what is mine, what was stolen from me. Fail to return and I will destroy you all!"

Stolen? Pax thought. *Am I keeping something that is not mine? My mother would never knowingly allow that to happen.*

Dhaal's words from earlier that day came rushing back:

Find peace in the clarity of facing a challenge in such obvious terms of white and black, of good and evil.

Pax looked over at Sören, who was lifting his hand and stepping forward, obviously ready to speak. One of the writhing arms shot outward and ensnared Sören, wrapping around his torso at a blinding speed. The arm was like some kind of rogue boa constrictor, and Sören was its prey. Sören was swept off of the ground and tossed through the air like a doll.

Pax stepped forward and started to yell for Sören, but before he could utter a word, Pax was also forcefully lifted off his feet and slammed to the ground. Stunned, but still conscious, he was aware of a deafening rush of air passing over him. His eyes stung from the grass and dirt in them.

His first thought was that Möbius had grabbed him with a snakelike arm, as he had with Sören. He felt up and down his body, squinting to look through his clouded vision, but did not see or feel any tentacles.

The sound was like that of a tornado, but Pax had never experienced one to appear so quickly. In the brief seconds that he struggled to regain his orientation and clear his vision, all became quiet and calm again.

Pax sat upright and wiped the grass and dirt from his face. His eyes watered profusely, but he could make out a trail of dirt and debris falling from the sky.

Möbius was nowhere in sight.

His exit had obviously been the cause of the sudden atmospheric disturbance. Pax marveled that their mysterious adversary commanded great force indeed.

The whole chain of events had such a surrealistic feel; from the startling arrival of Möbius, the conversation with this bizarre creature about the Artifex Temporis, and now his tumultuous exit – Pax could not help but wonder if this was some sort of dream.

He sat numbly, still staring upward as his vision painfully cleared. Rich black dirt and bits of the ravaged landscape slowly drifted down toward the earth, pushed by a gentle breeze that remained after the powerful gusts. A shout from Eckhardt shocked him to motion, and he stood quickly, scanning the scene for the source of the call for help.

There was a commotion from underneath a swirling pile of taupe canvas, which had only moments before stood as a tent. Pax trotted over toward the wrecked tent, where he was joined by Veronica, looking equally disheveled and dirty. Sören staggered over, rumpled and filthy. He had several large circular cuts in his shirt but was otherwise uninjured from his recent toss.

Sasha, Isaiah-Jung, and Agathi all made their way over to join Pax, Veronica, and Sören.

Eckhardt's head poked out from under a fold of heavy canvas as Pax and Isaiah-Jung lifted up a large panel of the weighty fabric. He still donned those strange goggles.

"Thanks, guys. I couldn't see a thing under there."

"Eck, maybe you should take off those silly goggles," Agathi snapped, clearly rattled. Everyone had always called him Eck since childhood. Even his mother called him Eck unless he was really in trouble; then she used his full name, even throwing in his middle name for serious offenses.

"Oh, yeah. Thanks. But if these worked, we will have some interesting images to study. Let me get back to my computer," Eckhardt said as he pulled the goggles from his head and jumped from the whirlpool of cloth. He dusted off his clothes and then took off running back toward the village without another word.

Pax shrugged and looked around at the group; it was typical Eckhardt behavior to disappear in flurry of excitement over some idea or discovery. Möbius apparently elicited more curiosity than fear from Eck.

"What do you make of that?" Veronica addressed the group. "Möbius looks like something from a nightmare." Her eyes were wide with an expression of helplessness.

"I wish it were just a bad dream." Pax replied. "I don't know what Möbius is - his appearance is alien, but there were certain things that seemed human as well. His voice was so clear, as was his English," Pax summarized.

"English? Möbius spoke in Dutch," Sören replied.

"Hebrew," said Isaiah-Jung.

"Russian," Sasha chimed in.

"Fascinating," said Pax. "We each heard in our own mother tongue. Like the story of Pentecost."

"The what?" Sasha asked.

Isaiah-Jung gave her a sideways glance, "I thought you had read everything, Sasha. It's from the Christian Bible," he commented, "when the Apostles started speaking languages they didn't know and the people listening each heard what they were saying in their own tongue."

"Interesting," said Sasha. "I do have several different versions; I'll have to read that."

"I think that's called *xenoglossy*," said Veronica. "You know, when you can speak a language you never learned. They also spoke *several* different languages they didn't know. Maybe that made the Apostles *xenoglossic polyglots?*"

"Okay, Veronica. Those are certainly fascinating semantics…" Pax said, scratching his head.

Veronica had always been the wordsmith of the group and her search for the meanings of words or her sharing of their definitions quite often led her off on just such tangents during a conversation. Veronica could continue on *ad infinitum* in her sharing information about the origin of a word or variations of pronunciation. Everyone knew this and typically found it endearing. In light of the gravity of their circumstances, they regarded this mental exercise as a mechanism to burn off some of her nervous energy resulting from fear and shock.

"But this is different. This Möbius knew what he was saying," Pax concluded, trying to redirect the focus of the discussion.

"Yes, you're right, Pax. Möbius wanted to make sure that we heard and understood his message. We can ponder the how and why later. We need to focus on what Möbius said," Sasha concluded.

"Möbius said he will destroy us if we do not hand over the watch, or whatever it was he called it," Sören said. "That part seems clear enough."

"And we are to make sure that he does not get it back. I do think we're going to need some help," Agathi said. "I did not know what to expect, but this was not it."

"Agathi, do you think you could catch up with Dhaal and tell him what happened? This might persuade him to return and help us," Pax asked.

"I was thinking the very same thing. Let me grab my pack and I'll take off. Veronica, you can have my share of lunch!" Agathi said.

"Where do you think Möbius comes from?" Sasha asked as she watched Agathi leave.

"From a long time away," Pax whispered quietly, remembering his mother's words from years before.

CHAPTER FOUR
(Parallel Dimensions)

A calming breeze met Dhaal as he moved peacefully across the expansive plain. Since his departure from Pax's Order of the Celestial Lotus, the sun had warmed his back and stretched his shadow out before him like a compass needle as he moved to the west. Several days walk from here he would turn north and make his way to the land of the Cyrills. He hoped to board a ship at the southernmost point of the Dark Sea that would carry him northward. If not, he would follow the shoreline on foot until he could find passage that would traverse the sea, dumping him in the Cyrillic Lands. These lands were more populated, and the roads more plentiful. He might even get really lucky and be able to catch one of the rare coal-burning trains that ran up into the colder regions.

His thoughts were interrupted by the peal of distant thunder. The old man stopped and surveyed the plain. The skies could not be any clearer, not a cloud in sight in any direction. As he looked toward the mountain, small flashes of violet light flashed against the pinkish-brown backdrop of the granite mountain range. Distinct fingers of electricity seemed to spray erratically from a point on the distance horizon and then dissipate.

As he stared intently, he felt a flush of heat move over him like a fever spreading uncontrollably. A flood of red appeared to flow over the mountain range and across the sky toward where Dhaal stood transfixed. In a matter of minutes, the heavens were blood red and the air was stifling, making it difficult to breathe. Smoke wafted up from the grass that surrounded him as the heat became more intense. Locusts rose up from the smoldering grass and flooded the sky, blocking the light and creating a deafening cacophony. The agitated insects flew erratically, striking Dhaal repeatedly in the face. His face burned and stung, but he could not raise his hands to ward off the feverish creatures. Soon, the insects began to burst into flames and fall to the earth in burning heaps. Dhaal could feel the heat through his robes and was certain the cloth of his garments was beginning to burn as well.

Acrid sulfur fumes seared his nostrils, and tears poured from his eyes. His lungs seized in pain as the toxic atmosphere weighed down on him like a crushing wave threatening to drown him. The sun moved at blazing speed through the blood redness of the sky and plunged behind the mountains. The moon burst through the hemorrhaging night, and many familiar constellations shone in the sky, the stars forming their mythical images, glowing intensely. As Dhaal recounted the names of each, the position of the stars began to shift; their relationships changed until totally new constellations shone in the heavens. Across the canvas of these new shapes, meteorites flew in reverse, exploding from the ground to disappear into the ether.

The moon faded away and a terrifying sight rose over the horizon. An enormous eye ascended to fill the sky. Dhaal was petrified by an ominous sensation of prescience, of seeing the future. The iris of the eye was like the blazing sun, eclipsed by the moon as a pupil. As the eye crested the mountain, it quickly receded into the distance, hovering over the horizon. Unblinking and malicious, this distant eye peered through time and space, cutting into Dhaal's soul to examine his innermost thoughts and deepest secrets. He stood paralyzed with fear and powerless to stop the eye's piercing gaze.

Dhaal awoke with a start, drenched in sweat. The sky was clear, and the sun had burned his face as it moved westward, tracing a path farther toward the horizon, now beginning its descent behind the mountain range. Dhaal had remained here for several hours. He scanned the ground and noticed it was indeed not littered with the charred carcasses of the incendiary locusts of his vision. His robe was intact and dripping with perspiration, quite the opposite of the burnt remnants in which he had been wearing in his dream. He saw no signs of violet light and heard no thunder.

The distant eye was nowhere in sight, but it had left an indelible mark in Dhaal's mind. This terrifying image would haunt him and be an uninvited traveling companion for the rest of his days. He thought the eye to be an allegory, but of what? The sky was clear again, but the sense of being watched from a distance was unnerving.

Dhaal wiped his brow and took a long drink from the water skin draped over his shoulder. Several hours had elapsed, and he was further behind schedule than before. He would have to ponder these visions while he trudged onward, trying to decide if these images held some clue or were just a fevered waste of precious time. He could appreciate the wisdom that came with his age but often questioned the behavior of the aging body and mind. Dhaal shook his head and began walking.

He focused on a distant landmark; a few ancient stone columns rose up out of the sweeping grasses in various states of disrepair. Only one pitted and chipped column was complete, with a small section of an arch still gracing the top, a curving stone arm reaching off into nowhere, grasping out to a section of history. The bases of two other columns peered over the grasses, and those few pieces made up the ruins in their entirety. Dhaal searched his memory to determine what deity or epic battle these columns had been constructed to honor, but came up with nothing. He thought they were Doric columns and guessed they must have been standing for over seven thousand years. Fluting, once prominent, was now worn smooth by time. Dhaal was amazed, thinking how these stone columns had stood through several world wars, centuries of severe weather, ancient battles fought hand to hand, and countless earthquakes. The history these columns represented was breathtaking to him, even though the specific events surrounding them remained unknown.

A small pond cut a swath through the green grass before the columns; a shimmering portrait of the stone columns danced on its silvery surface.

Dhaal had not walked but a few meters when he heard a lilting voice calling from behind.

"Dhaal!"

Turning, he saw sunlight glinting off of golden strands of hair and quickly realized that it was Agathi in the distance, navigating through the heavy, waist-high grass field that separated the two. The lush green blades parted like water as the spry young woman pushed forward. Agathi was almost as tall as Veronica but had never been considered gangly. She was fond of hiking, running, and climbing. Agathi was very strong and had the muscles to prove it. Sasha had described Agathi as "Botticelliesque" based on a picture she had found in one of her many books. Agathi thought the image of the woman in the painting was beautiful, and blushed at the comparison.

Dhaal could not help but wonder as he watched her approach if the purpose for his waking dream had been to delay his progress so Agathi could catch up to him. He felt with certainty this was indeed one purpose but that more information was hidden within the allegorical vision.

"I'm so glad I found you!" Agathi said as she bent over, out of breath, and rested her hands on her knees. She lifted one hand and placed it on Dhaal's forearm. "I wasn't even sure if I was headed in the right direction."

"Much longer and you would have been stranded out here in the dark," Dhaal said as he gestured toward the last remnant of the sun above the horizon.

"That's all right. I love it out here," she replied, "I thought you'd have traveled farther by now. I figured I'd have to spend at least one night away, so I'm prepared." Agathi pulled the rucksack from her back and showed Dhaal. A beautifully woven gray wool blanket was neatly rolled and tied to the pack. The coarse fabric was graced with an undulating blue design at each end, framing intermittent red and yellow alchemical symbols. Also attached was a small water skin. The neatness of the pack left no doubt in the older man's mind that everything else she needed was contained inside.

"It's a pleasant surprise, but I didn't expect to see you again so soon." Dhaal tilted his head and opened his hands in the same wide gesture she had seen when they had first met. It was an oddly comforting stance.

"Pax wanted me to let you know that the enemy has arrived, and it's not human." Agathi looked seriously at Dhaal.

The afternoon sunlight warmed her cheeks and illuminated her striking turquoise eyes but could not evaporate the fear and shock that visibly lingered after her encounter with the enemy.

"Out of nowhere this creature just appeared, and what a weird sight! It was a mixture of human, animal, and machine," Agathi explained, gesticulating wildly. "It had long tentacles and just floated there in midair.

"It spoke to us, and called itself Möbius. It told Pax that he had seven days to present the watch he is protecting. Otherwise …" she trailed off and made a helpless gesture. Her hair, which reminded Dhaal of corn silk, had fallen down over her face. Agathi ran both hands through it in an unconscious movement, creating a rough part down the middle and once again revealing her face.

"We should make camp," Dhaal said. "I can see I'm not destined to move farther today. Let's move over near those columns by the pond," he said, pointing.

Within minutes, the two arrived at the ruins. Dhaal removed his bag and began walking in circles to tamp down the tall grass. Agathi followed his lead. "Just like my cat when she's ready to take a nap!" she said, smiling.

The weather was warm even as the sun moved toward setting, and the sky was clear. The two opted not to bother setting up their tents, preferring instead to see a wonderful ceiling of stars they knew would emerge out here on these plains, far away from the evening lights of the village.

There were several empty fire pits that had been roughly constructed of small stones, but plant life piercing through the charred wood and ash told that it had indeed been some time since anyone had passed this way. Dhaal cleared one of the pits close by and built a small fire, where he brewed black tea for both. Between the two sharing what they carried in their packs, they feasted on a dinner of pumpernickel bread, dried lamb, persimmons, and some dry salty beans, which Dhaal produced from a thick paper bag.

Agathi continued to describe Möbius in great detail and told Dhaal about how each had heard him speak in their mother tongue. She repeatedly remarked as to the surreal feeling of the whole encounter.

Dhaal sat listening intently, asking questions at various points.

"Möbius called the device by a strange name," Agathi told Dhaal, "the Artifex Tempo ... Temponus ..."

"The Artifex Temporis?" Dhaal asked.

"That's it!" Agathi answered.

"The Time Maker," Dhaal said. "This is one of the strange stories I first heard while in the lands far south of the Zeitlos, the lands about which you asked me earlier today.

"The name *Artifex Temporis* is Latin, a language dead for millennia, so I translate loosely because I am by no means an expert." Dhaal shook his head.

"The tale I heard told was of a tool from the gods that allowed the one possessing this object to move freely through time, future and past, changing the events of history on a whim. As a youth, such stories were amazing and mysterious, fodder for the imagination!" the elderly man said, wide-eyed. "But my father said such stories were the talk of idle fools, tales from men who dreamt of changing their past because they did nothing in the present.

"Möbius believes that the Artifex is real and is in Pax's possession," Dhaal concluded.

"Then Möbius could alter time as he saw fit? So all of this is about time travel?" Agathi asked. "I didn't think that was possible."

"I think Möbius desires immortality," Dhaal responded.

"When he appeared, he said he was eternal," Agathi recounted.

"I'm not sure why I say 'he.' Nothing about such an abomination resembled anything truly human, except those eyes," Agathi trailed off. "And his hands and voice were those of a man. I guess that's why."

"Möbius also said he sees all; he would have you believe all these things, but they are clearly not true. But we cannot dismiss the dangerous potential of Möbius just because he distorts the facts. I don't believe any of us had any inkling of the value of the object that

Pax holds, the Artifex Temporis. But who knows! If Möbius gains control of this device, maybe his delusions will become reality."

"Possibly Möbius speaks of what he sees in the future?" Agathi said.

Dhaal tilted his head and raised an eyebrow, conveying that it could be the case, but that it was doubtful.

"What exactly is time travel?" Agathi asked. She had always thought of it as a flight of fancy, but after Möbius's appearance, such strange ideas seemed disturbingly more possible.

"That's quite a question, and I am neither a mathematician nor a quantum physicist," Dhaal started, "but I guess we all become philosophers as we get older," he chuckled.

"You are obviously familiar with the space within which you move each day. You know that objects have width, height, and depth; you know that you travel from one point to another. The ancient mathematician Euclid described these in terms of x, y, and z; this is three-dimensional Euclidean space. Euclid set up the framework for more dimensions beyond these three."

Dhaal moved his hands through the air, clearly drawing the shape of a box.

"If you are a fan of mathematics, consider that you travel across this Euclidean space, viewing this space as did Pythagoras," Dhaal started scribbling equations in the sand.

He continued on, and Agathi recognized almost all of the symbols but did not comprehend any meaning from what Dhaal wrote.

"You know it takes you a certain amount of time to travel from one place to another, from here over to the Zeitlos, for example." The old man motioned to where they sat, and then pointed to the mountain range in the distance. "Let's call that time t, or the fourth dimension.

So we now have *x,y,z*, and *t*. These make up the construct of space and time. They are linked together forming a continuum, a group of things that are inseparable."

The elderly man paused and took a deep breath; his eyes scanned the skies, taking in the beauty of the lingering dusk before returning his focus to Agathi.

"We measure time as linear, in only one direction," Dhaal continued on. "This doesn't really address the nature of time at all, merely it's passing. If there were no clocks or watches, time would still pass, and its effect on our physical world would be equally visible.

"Think of time as more of a fluid, flowing within the physical three dimensions, like water in an infinite box. Think of being able to jump between the physical points of x, y, and z by folding the distance between and being able to go forward or backward or even sideways. That is how I envision the traveling of the time-space continuum to which Möbius referred."

Agathi sat mesmerized by Dhaal. She was obviously interested and seemed to readily comprehend his teaching. This was all very challenging, but she was thrilled when he decided to share more of what he knew on the subject.

"Of course, you can imagine the philosophical conflicts this brings up. The classic is the grandfather paradox, which questions what would happen if someone traveled back in time and prevented their own grandfather and grandmother from meeting, or even worse ..." Dhaal trailed off. Agathi was young and he did not want to be too graphic or morbid in his definitions and descriptions.

"Then the time-traveler would have never been born, and hence could not travel back in time. Or the salvation paradox, which questions what would happen if you traveled back in time and saved someone who would have otherwise perished. Then, what if that person went on to produce subsequent generations that did not exist at the time of retrograde time travel? What effect would the presence of all these new individuals have on the present?" Dhaal paused to let these ideas sink in.

"What is retrograde?" Agathi asked.

"Retrograde just means to go backward," Dhaal explained.

As Dhaal continued to speak, images suddenly exploded across Agathi's vision; she was actually picturing the concepts Dhaal explained in physical form before her eyes. A sense of liberation flowed through her, as if someone was handing to her the keys to the secrets of the universe.

As quickly as the sensation of enlightenment had appeared, it disappeared, and the concepts once again seemed overwhelming. But Agathi could not escape that she had seen into the infinite; that she had been given a glimpse into eternity. She knew then, that the memory of this sensation would always be with her.

Agathi became aware of Dhaal's voice once again. "There is the Temporal Protection Principle, which states that what does not exist at the time of retrograde time travel cannot be created in the past. Then, there's the corollary that states.."

"Wait! Wait!" Agathi waved her hands and shook her head. "This is too much for now.

"That is all very amazing Dhaal, but it's too much to take in all at one time. I need to think these through," Agathi said. "You could drive yourself insane considering all of the implications of time travel."

"I think many have," said Dhaal. "Anyway, these are just theories and principles that attempt to explain the physical world; theories don't create reality. I often wonder if the finite human mind can even comprehend an infinite universe. That's why I choose to focus on the present," he smiled.

Dusk softly blanketed the two in soft lilac hues as they sat without talking. After some time, Agathi broke the silence.

"Okay. So, Möbius wants the watch so that he can travel in time."

"Möbius obviously believes that the Artifex Temporis is truly the key to time travel," Dhaal concurred.

"But even if it is possible, how would the Artifex help him do this; how would someone actually achieve time travel?" Agathi asked in a very pragmatic tone. She had regained her focus after the pause in their discussion, and was once again ready to tackle the questions surrounding their mysterious visitor.

"That is difficult for me to comprehend," Dhaal replied. "I understand that as you travel, the closer you travel to the speed of light, the less you age. But you've seen me trudging across these fields at a snail's pace. I obviously have no clue as how to move at such speeds," he laughed and his cheeks flushed.

Agathi was once more engulfed in thought. "So if I could travel into space at the speed of light, I could stay gone for what seemed like a year, return, and no time would have passed?"

"As I understand the theory," the older man replied.

"Travel to the future in very small increments seems easier to grasp than moving backward in time," Dhaal carried on, "I believe the main possible gateway for such travel is a *wormhole*, a tunnel created by warping the continuity of space-time."

Dhaal leaned over and sketched out a grid on the ground that Agathi took to be a flat surface. He then drew an identical grid in such a way that it was clear that there were two grids, one on top of the other.

"Think of these the same physical space separated by some period of time," Dhaal stated. "Now connect these two by a small tunnel pulled from the fabric of each grid."

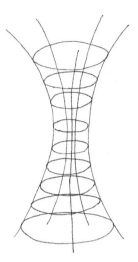

A wireframe tunnel appeared between the two grids and connected them together.

"If you had an engine that could propel you fast enough into one end of this tunnel and then move toward the other, time would appear to travel much slower inside the tunnel than outside. With such a propulsion system, one could move through the tunnel without time passing and emerge onto the plane at the other end, where a significant amount of time would have passed."

"The longer the wormhole, the more time would pass," Agathi commented.

"And the more powerful a propulsion system you would need to move between one opening and the other," Dhaal reflected.

Night had set in while they had been talking, and the stars shone brightly above. Purple flashes once again appeared in the distance, capturing Dhaal's attention. In the darkness of night, the electrostatic bursts lit up the plain and reflected off of the mountains. Dhaal's awareness was heightened, and he noticed he was breathing rapidly. He willed his body to slow his respiration and control the fear that accelerated his heart.

A low rumble followed each violet burst, and the smell of ozone quickly filled the air. Stars faded and disappeared as clouds coalesced in the sky.

"We must hide," Dhaal told Agathi as he stood. He picked up her rucksack and reached for her hand.

As he moved to help Agathi stand, the whole area was suddenly engulfed in a cocoon of blinding purple light. Dhaal could feel the static electricity pouring over him and the smell of ozone burned in his nose. As swiftly as it had appeared, the light disappeared, leaving Dhaal and Agathi somewhat dazed and disoriented.

A large splash in the pond caught Agathi's attention. It looked as if something large had been thrown into the water from the shore; a huge fan of water sprayed off to one side, and a massive wake spread across the surface. White foam roiled, and a figure suddenly lunged upwards out of the water.

Even in the nighttime, with only the starlight and the light of the moon from above, the pair could see that the figure in the water was massive. Neither Agathi nor Dhaal had ever seen a human that large. Driving powerful legs up and down, the giant charged through the water, heading toward the shoreline closest to where they stood, gaping.

Several more pulses of light flashed behind the columns, depositing two more massive figures. As Agathi glanced back and forth between the giant pushing to reach the edge of the pond and the two now marching toward them from behind the columns, she began to move backward.

Thankful for at least the minor interference provided by the columns, Agathi was shocked as she watched one of the leviathan men slam his bare forearm against the stone pillar. The man didn't fall to the ground in pain as she expected; her breath escaped her as the column itself began to teeter. One more strike and the column broke apart into three segments and toppled over. The small segment of the arch top struck the second man's shoulder in a glancing blow, but did not seem to even slow his forward progress. Agathi guessed that such a block of marble weighed hundreds of pounds and could not imagine that the man had not been crushed by such weight.

Now very scared, Agathi started to turn and run but found she could not. Two large hands held her shoulders, and while she could not turn enough to get a glimpse of her captor, she felt certain that this too was one of these giants. She instinctively slammed her elbow backward, hoping to find the person's solar plexus and free herself.

Her elbow painfully struck metal. A large hand clamped around her meager wrist, pulling her arm behind her and pinning it firmly against her back; Agathi could not move.

Another burst of violet light engulfed them, forcing Agathi to hold her breath and tightly close her eyes. When the violet light dissipated, the moonlight, grass, pond, and columns were all gone. Agathi stood in very dim, gray light, and found it difficult to focus on her surroundings.

The pain in her elbow exploded as she was lifted up onto her toes and moved forward. She winced but did not call out. Instead, she closed her eyes tightly, trying to regain her vision in the dimness. When she opened them again, she could see Dhaal hunched over about ten meters away, facing her, his arm firmly in the grasp of one of the giants.

Agathi felt very peculiar, almost as if she were somehow lighter. The muscles in her legs were cramping and burned as if from intense physical activity. Her hands and feet tingled painfully, and she stood opening and closing her hands until the sensation began to subside.

Even though she was being held securely, Agathi shifted her weight side to side until she was comfortable that her legs would respond if and when the opportunity arose. It took longer for her to try and adjust to what it was she was actually seeing. They were clearly somewhere else. She did not recognize this area and wondered if she had been knocked unconscious for some time while they had traveled to this place, but she really did not think so. She had no headache and was not groggy like the time she had collided into a heavy door and not regained consciousness for several hours. In fact, she felt that her senses were operating *hyper acutely,* that her perception was in fact *better* than usual. She decided this sensation could be a byproduct of fear.

As Agathi's eyes pierced through the dim gray light, she could see that she and Dhaal were encircled by at least four of these armored beings, each towering over them by more than a meter. She examined the giant that stood next to her more closely. The skin was very ashen and the facial features angular. Each of the giants had long ink-black hair, with some of the hair pulled back into a queue. Their eyes were elongated with a slight epicanthic fold similar to one of Agathi's own close friends, common to those who hailed from the Distant East. What was not common was that their irises were bleach white and reflected the dim light very brightly, almost as if they glowed from an energy source within. The sclera of their eyes was a deep, dark black like their hair, but wet and glistening. Agathi had seen wolves with eyes like this before; they had always been the most vicious.

Studying the three she could see, she realized that their features were not just similar, they were exactly identical. Never before had Agathi seen such identical replicates of an individual occur in nature. Dopplegänger was the only appropriate word Agathi could find to describe this; she decided that all of these giants must be clones from a single source. Their dress was also very similar; each wore a copper cuirass, or breastplate, and some wore heavy boots with armored plates on the front. The one holding Dhaal, apparently the one that had initially landed in the pond, stood dripping with water and wore no boots at all, it's feet covered only by the same material that made up the pants.

Agathi tried to imagine why such giants of immense strength needed armor and wondered who would be foolish enough to enter into combat with such formidable beings. Even more so, she wondered where these monstrous men came from. Could they have come up from the lands south of the Zeitlos-Granit? Agathi had heard stories of fierce warriors from those unknown regions but never of such a race of beings as stood around her.

Everything initially seemed to be in shades of gray; the light was very dim. As she strained to focus, Agathi started to discern muted colors— faded watercolor washes of pale hues. She was struck by the overall lack of sensation of the environment; it did not feel warm or cool and there was no air moving. Wherever they were felt stagnant; it felt like... *nothing*.

Low-hanging clouds spread as far as the eye could see, like rain clouds just before a storm, dense and gray, but also soft and diffuse. The clouds did not seem to move at all or change.

The dopplegänger that restrained Dhaal lifted him from the ground and carried him closer to Agathi. The old man was clinging desperately to his walking staff and grimaced when the giant lowered him back to the ground -Agathi feared he had been hurt badly during their abduction. The soldier released Dhaal's left arm, and the older man immediately hunched over, his breathing shallow and raspy. After a few moments, he stood upright, intently eyeing the stoic giants. There were muffled words shared between them; one appeared to be giving instructions or orders, the other nodding in response. Dhaal immediately labeled the silent nodding one as lower in rank, a soldier. Dhaal watched this soldier closely. After he had received his orders and been dismissed, he reached up and made adjustments to a dial located on the upper right of the cuirass he wore. A needle moved on the dial. He then depressed the face of the dial and the whole assembly moved inward.

The soldier immediately disappeared in a flash of violet light.

Dhaal blinked hard, trying to make sure he had seen correctly. The soldier was nowhere in sight. Dhaal glanced at Agathi, but she was focusing on the leader, who had turned to face her, apparently speaking to the colossus who held her arms. Agathi strained to understand the exchange between these two, but the language these strange giants spoke was unintelligible to her.

Dhaal looked at each of the soldiers that he could see, and saw the glowing dial present on the breastplate of each.

The hands that held Agathi were cold and clammy; that sensation made her more uncomfortable than the fact she was being held against her will.

Agathi looked up at Dhaal, who was only a few feet away, looking for signs of bleeding or other injury. As she looked at him, the old man's head suddenly fell forward, and he slumped to the ground. The enormous figure let him fall. Agathi panicked and tried to move toward Dhaal but could not; the soldier's grip was far too strong. As she looked down at the old man, he suddenly sprang up to his feet!

In a flurry of well-planned and practiced motion, he whirled around, spinning his walking stick and then driving it upward into the chin of the giant who had held him captive only seconds before.

Dhaal then rapidly dropped into a horse stance without waiting to see what damage he had inflicted, and immediately launched into another attack with the staff, butting the other end of the stick below the upraised right arm of the stunned captor.

Agathi was amazed. Dhaal had obviously been faking his injury so as to lower the soldier's guard and awareness. What Dhaal had not yet seen was that his first blow had completely knocked the head off of the giant that had held him. Literally,

Dhaal's staff had struck directly under the soldier's chin and driven it upward.

And it kept on going off his shoulders, through the air, and into the darkness. Where the bizarre face had been was a sight all too similar to what she had seen earlier in the day: a clear structure with a spinning object mysteriously floating within. There were no eyes this time, and the geometry was different. The head of this robot, or hybrid, or whatever it was that Sören had called Möbius, was an inverted cone, growing larger from the shoulders upward. And inside was a smaller, spinning cylinder.

Dhaal's second strike had loosened the cuirass protecting the creature's chest, dropping it to the ground along with the entire covering of the right arm. Beneath the copper armor was a metallic ribcage, protecting a clear tank. Inside the tank was housed a mechanical assembly rife with gears of varying size and design. The same bluish fluid partially filled this cavity, covering these mechanics and sloshing about freely.

Now only a metal skeleton remained from the waist up, with the exception of the left arm, which still appeared human.

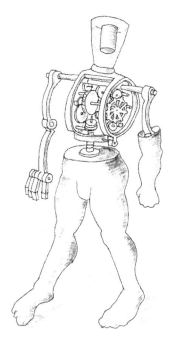

Dhaal dropped onto the ground and grabbed the cuirass and began very intently doing something that Agathi could not make out. In a matter of seconds, he was back on his feet, holding the cuirass over his shoulder. He took a step toward Agathi and was extending his hand, when the robot, now exposed and devoid of his pseudo-human covering, lashed out and drove Dhaal to the ground by jamming his fist into the center of the elderly man's back. The motion looked harsh and uncoordinated.

Agathi watched as Dhaal looked up at her. He was in pain, and it was clear that he could not reach her. The robot began to move toward him. Dhaal quickly weighed his options.

"I'll come back for you," Dhaal said as he drove his fist downward against a dial on the upper portion of the metal corselet. Agathi started to answer him, but he vanished before she could speak.

The being that had been holding Agathi immediately released her and moved quickly over to his damaged counterpart, pushing Agathi aside. No doubt Dhaal's disappearance was completely unexpected and causing confusion between those left behind.

Agathi took advantage of the chaos and their temporary loss of interest in her and quietly moved backward, away from these strange creatures. She kept her focus intently on the cluster of clones before her. They had not returned their attention to Agathi, so she turned and ran as fast as she could into the dark gray veil before her. She had no idea in which direction she headed, but as long as it was away from those giants, it was where she wanted to go.

Agathi felt anxious and scared, but a sense of power and agility consumed her, which she attributed to adrenalin. Whatever the source of this power, all Agathi knew was that she was moving away from these dopplegängers, and at a high rate of speed.

CHAPTER FIVE
(An Evil Genius)

Bonaventure R. Golding III stood staring at the mound of papers he held within his hands, crumpled beneath his grip and damp from the sweat of his palms. He ripped the stack in two and threw the shreds to the floor. These papers stated that all research in the area of hybrid organic processors would be immediately stopped unless a successful system was included in the next planned launch. He would be forced to cease and desist his research due to the "anomalous and erratic performance of the Somatic Kernels, as well as the public outcry concerning the ethics of the program."

Dr. Golding stood quietly but shook with rage.

"Cancel my research? These people can't even comprehend the work I am doing!" he hissed through clenched teeth, staring at Thornton Daunnier. The hatred in his eyes was unmistakable. Thornton Daunnier was but one in a cadre of lawyers retained by the Board of

Directors at the Institute for Artificial Cerebral Development. He was not yet even forty, which made him the youngest partner in the history of the firm. Being aggressive and willing to win at any cost, he was regularly selected to perform the unsavory jobs for the firm. As a result, Daunnier had already seen a response like Golding's many times over his brief career.

"Bonaventure," Daunnier responded, "we both know that there is no public outcry over the ethics of this project. The Board of Directors is just getting nervous over the ..." Daunnier paused, rolling his eyes, "over the disturbing reports they've received about the function of SomKern4, and with the idiosyncrasies developing in the other units."

"It's Dr. Golding to you," Golding glared at the lawyer, "And the public knows nothing of the fourth unit."

The Board had unanimously voted to host Dr. Bonaventure Golding III fifteen years ago when his groundbreaking research was bringing money into the Institute like a tidal wave. They had coordinated record-setting research grants for the development of the Deep Space Colonization project. But even considering the amazing medical breakthroughs that he had accomplished using microprocessors in brain surgery, the Somatic Kernel was not materializing as fast as anyone had hoped. The Board had grown tired of project delays and a steady stream of requests for more funding. Finally, they had used "public outcry" as their basis to threaten Dr. Golding to produce results and to protect themselves from the public should anything go terribly wrong with any portion of the space program that had their name on it.

"The work you've done surgically implanting processors to cure people is amazing," Daunnier continued as he squatted down to pick up the crumpled shreds of the document that Golding had destroyed in a rage. His new leather shoes squeaked in protest as he stood back up.

"If you can't produce a functioning unit before the next launch, you can just rest on those laurels for a while," Daunnier suggested. "There are others waiting in line to take over the research on the Somatic Kernel. Bonaventure Golding III can just fade away as the historical figure that started the program, leaving it to others to perfect. The Institute just won't be footing the bill."

The Somatic Kernel was the first successful integration of the human brain and an array of powerful computer processors. All of the early development prototypes using mice were still functioning beautifully after almost seven years, far beyond the life expectancy of about two years for *Mus musculus*, the common house mouse.

Golding had theorized that the brain was not subject to the same effects of aging if placed into a controlled environment outside of the body; the mice brains had proved his theory beyond question. Years before, he had teamed with Dr. Jonas Mercurio Goethe, the surgeon who early into the twenty-third century had performed the world's first successful human brain transplant. Dr. Goethe always said that it was really a full body transplant since the consciousness and personality more reflected that of the donor brain than of the recipient body.

The success of this duo quickly blossomed into a fruitful partnership, although it had become immediately clear to Dr. Goethe that Bonaventure Golding was a superior and unique intellect, absolutely the most brilliant man he had ever known. Dr. Golding, as it were, had foibles equal to the level of his intelligence, but Goethe was able to overlook those idiosyncrasies by focusing on the great possibilities of scientific achievement that he envisioned them producing. Frequently, some red flag or another popped up in terms of Golding's personality or bizarre scientific proposals, but Goethe trudged on nonetheless, burying his head deeper in the sand, awaiting fame and success.

Golding and Goethe started a company together as an offshoot of their research. Seat of Consciousness Inc. was a business designed to store a person's memories onto a chip so that those memories could be restored or retrieved at any time. The technology was fascinating but did not prove very useful. The memories could indeed be transferred back from the chip to the brain, but the original association to a particular memory could not. For example, seeing an old photo of a family member would lead to the recall of a totally unrelated event, such as a sound or a smell that had no association with the photograph.

Nevertheless, the research that had gone into this venture proved very useful in the early development of the Somatic Kernel and to robotics in general.

The addition of an organic brain had been the missing link in the development of robotics over the years; without the emotional component and the free association of which a natural brain was capable, true independently operating robots would never be possible, Golding had theorized. He designed a platform to house the brain, which acted as the central sensory controller. When the brain encountered more difficult questions or tasks that required higher processing capabilities, it would simply direct those to one of the many computer processors idly waiting in an integrated array.

Golding explained to the general public that it was just like a normal human being who used a computer; they move through their day without straining the limits of their intelligence for most things and then rely on computers for more complex tasks, taking the results from the system to factor into a final decision, only trillions of times faster in his arrangement. His flowery speech drew images of his research leading one day soon to the average person being able to receive computer implants to give them instantaneous access to super mental processing power.

Such a thought was truly revolting to Dr. Golding. He thought it would be a waste to offer such a gift to the mass of humanity. "Pearls before swine," he had muttered to himself when penning this talk. He simply needed them to cooperate and fund his research, and dangling such a carrot before their dull and average lives seemed like the perfect incentive.

In talking of his research, Dr. Bonaventure Golding III neglected to mention that the human brains in his original experiments did not respond well to being removed from their body and placed in a sterile environment, devoid of their usual stimulation. In simple terms, the brain suffered from debilitating boredom. Without a body; without any receptors or sources of input, the brains had simply stopped functioning.

The issue of sleep had also been a major problem. Dr. Golding's team had spent years trying to address the issue of sleep by regulating hormones and adjusting the controlled environment, but to no avail. Their final solution had been to eliminate sleep altogether by providing a constant supply of serotonin, a neurotransmitter that seemed to eliminate the need for sleep. Initially, this looked like a successful approach, but several of the researchers voiced concerns over the long-term effects of this tactic.

Three Somatic Kernels had been functioning for over a year now under these new conditions, and Dr. Golding had taken every opportunity to make sure the news media and public were aware of this. Concerns over the latest theory du jour that the sun could be going supernova within the next few hundred years had fueled the public interest in the Deep Space Colonization project. The Somatic Kernel fit perfectly into this scheme, because it essentially provided a human being to control the ship that would carry cargoes of hundreds of human beings, animals, and food, suspended in cryogenic storage—a human being that never grew tired or suffered the ravages of growing old. The general public seemed much more comfortable subjecting their well-being to another human, even though disembodied, than they did to a computer.

Dr. Golding had also neglected to mention that he had begun to observe displays of various degrees of psychosis a few months into the project. Delirium, paranoia, and eventually complete insanity had disabled Somatic Kernel Four, or SomKern4, as listed on the unit's chart. Fortunately, this had been detected before going public with the project, so the public only knew of the three units, all of which were reported to be functioning normally. He knew his idea would work if just given time; it was only a matter of screening for better brains. If he could only convince a scholar, someone with a strong intellect to participate, he knew it would work. Golding could not understand why no one would volunteer. "You could become immortal!" he had shouted at one researcher as they ran out of his office one day after Golding had tried to solicit his cooperation.

"The launch is scheduled for sometime within three months or so, I believe," Golding said, looking at the date on his watch. "Just give me a little more time, Mr. Daunnier. Please. I just need to find a strong intellectual brain." Golding was trying a more rational approach. "Convince the Board that the Somatic Kernel will be worth trillions of dollars to them as part of the Colonization Program, which means billions for you as well, I would think."

Golding could see the wheels turning in the young man's head. The lawyer's eyes had a distant look, and Golding could sense the effect of his words on the younger man. Bonaventure himself did not particularly understand material greed, but full well understood how to use it to manipulate those afflicted by the condition. Dangling the appropriate carrot was easy, and typically carrots in the form of gilded items or cold hard cash produced the quickest results.

"Well, for now you have until the next launch of the Deep-Space Colonization Project." He crossed his arms and stared at the floor. "But if you fail, perhaps I could be motivated to try and convince them to fund you for a while longer."

He's leaving the door open to blackmail me if I fail, Golding thought in disgust.

"You'll need to make some progress, and quickly. These are not patient men," Daunnier concluded.

"Progress will be quick," Golding said absentmindedly.

Staring at the notice, he decided that he needed to call Dr. Goethe immediately. Golding did not even notice as Thornton Daunnier walked from the room.

He had an idea that would save the project.

His idea had the added benefit of allowing him to live forever.

CHAPTER SIX
(Doubts)

Pax sat motionless on the hillside above Orneth. Deep furrows creased his forehead. His eyes stared out over the village but saw only the events of the recent past. He had stolen away into the steppes to sit and think alone for a while.

Tall grasses spread across the rolling hills like the soft fur of a sleeping animal and swayed gently in the evening breeze. These thin blades of green and brown worked in unison to hide Pax from the view of anyone casually surveying the scene.

A sensation that he had a sibling had always haunted Pax. He knew that his father had disappeared shortly after his birth, but he always felt he was a twin. For fear that something tragic might have happened at their birth, he never pursued this intuition with his mother, not wanting to cause her any more pain if that had indeed been the case.

This feeling was always present but surfaced more intensely when he spent time alone in introspective thought.

The appearance of Möbius and all of the proceeding events plagued Pax; an oppressive sense of responsibility for placing his friends at risk gnawed at his conscience. Möbius appeared to be a powerful force, with an army of powerful soldiers at his command. Had Pax set them all up for failure?

"What have I done?" he said aloud, finally stirring from the statuesque position in which he had remained for hours.

"You've done what was right," a soft voice answered.

Pax turned, startled. Veronica sat only a meter way, resting her chin in the cleft formed between her knees. He decided that she had been sitting there for some time. Her eyes were pools of violet, softened by concern. She smiled, but it was a gentle smile, one that did not brighten her face or bring the usual twinkle to her eye. Pax thought he noticed a glint of light from moisture on her cheeks and guessed that she had recently been crying.

Not sure what else to say, Pax blurted out, "Hi, Veronica. How long have you been here?"

"Long enough. Maybe an hour or so. Remember, I don't have a watch," she joked quietly.

Veronica had her hair pulled back into a loose ponytail that pooled on the ground behind her and flowed over in a wave of henna to cover her feet.

Pax thought how beautiful she was, and that made his soul ache even more. Why had he endangered all of those whom he held dear, most of all Veronica?

He had never really expressed his feelings toward Veronica; in reality, he was just beginning to realize the meaning of such feelings and to admit them to himself. They had been lifelong friends, as had most of the group, but Veronica had always been special. Pax had not delved into his own heart concerning how he thought Veronica might feel about him, although he desperately hoped she shared his sentiments.

His doubt about Veronica's feelings toward him was swept away by the wash of amber light that flowed over her face in the approaching twilight. The expression of concern and emotion was unmistakable.

Pax felt his face flush and hoped that Veronica could not see his reddening cheeks in the light of dusk.

Almost as if Veronica were reading all of these thoughts in Pax's head like pages in a book, she slid over in the grass beside him and put her head on his shoulder.

"Pax, none of this is your fault. We've all known for years that there would be some sort of confrontation," she said with quiet conviction.

"Veronica, you can't tell me that any of us expected anything like *this*," he said, tilting his head toward hers. "I still can't believe what I saw. I was sitting here for a while pondering if I had gone insane."

An expression moved quickly across Veronica's face and disappeared. Pax gathered that the same thought and self-doubt might have passed through her mind as well.

"No, I wouldn't tell you that anyone expected anything like Möbius; I think we were all waiting for a bad man to come and try to steal the Artifex. But it doesn't matter; we know that we are friends and that we will face that unknown together. And that's what we all intend to do," she said calmly.

Pax closed his eyes and was once again thankful that she could not see his face. With all of the emotions coursing through his veins, his feelings were brimming just below the surface, and he did not want Veronica staring at him should they spill over as tears.

He could not escape from admitting to himself that Veronica was the reason for many of these conflicting emotions and that he was so glad that she was here with him now.

"I don't know what I would do if anything happened to anyone," Pax said. He added, "To you."

Looking down as her head rested on his shoulder, he could tell from her cheeks that a smile spread across Veronica's face. He had added the words as an afterthought, but they both knew that was all he had really wanted to say.

Nighttime coolness crept across the damp grass, chasing the last whispers of daylight over the horizon. Pax and Veronica sat in silence, enjoying each other's warmth and watching the stars slowly appear above.

CHAPTER SEVEN
(Time Travel?)

"We've trained for years, developing our fighting skills as well as our armor," Sören spoke to Pax and Veronica, "but neither are any match for something like Möbius and the legions he promised to bring when he returns."

"We'll just have to fight another way," replied Pax as he stared intently at a small crucible currently engulfed in flames. Molten gold swirled within. "Hopefully this will throw him off a bit and buy us some time."

Veronica worked gently. She was delicately removing the Artifex Temporis from a plaster casting she had made.

"What are you doing?" Sören asked.

"Making a fake Artifex," Pax spoke as he focused on a brilliant stream of gold pouring into Veronica's casting. "With a surprise inside."

"Our parents might be a little upset when they realize we borrowed some old gold trinkets to melt down," Veronica smiled.

"But I guess that's a small price to pay for saving the world," she concluded.

"Time to figure out how to really fight Möbius," Pax said. "If he is really dependent on a mechanical device like the Artifex, he might be subject to the same limitations of such devices."

"You believe that a being like Möbius that can possibly travel in time can really be crippled by not having the Artifex? How can something driven by gears and springs be so important?" Sören sounded skeptical.

"Möbius does seem extremely concerned over this golden watch, or whatever the Artifex is," Veronica replied. "But Pax hasn't observed anything particularly special about this thing over the years he's held onto it," she continued.

"That's true," Sören agreed.

"Besides, Eckhardt's working on some different ideas, a parallel approach," Pax said.

"He visited the college research lab and got some samples of various viruses that affect marine organisms. He plans to make what he called 'viral mortars.'

"Eckhardt believes that if Möbius's tentacles are real or are engineered from the DNA of an actual cephalopod—a squid or an octopus—that he could be vulnerable to the diseases that target them," Veronica said.

"He also picked up on the frequency on which Möbius spoke. Apparently, what we heard was also broadcast at various radio frequencies and wirelessly onto the network that Eck set up for us. Eckhardt thinks Möbius didn't know how to best communicate with us, so he tried several methods.

"And they all worked. But I guess that means Möbius doesn't actually 'know all and see all,'" Pax commented with a sense of hopeful sarcasm.

"Eck's using some of the malicious code he's collected, and some that he's written himself, and wants to try and transmit that in hopes of infecting the software component of Möbius, if indeed there is one.

"Möbius must contain the hardware to broadcast radio transmissions as well as to produce audible sound, and the software to translate these signals onto our network," Veronica continued.

"He's a regular communications satellite," Pax agreed.

"Eck called what he is making a viral beacon, or something like that," said Veronica as she handed the Artifex Temporis back to Pax.

He held it in his palm and studied it closely. Every time he looked at this device, he discovered something new or different. He realized that he found it comforting to have it back. Even though Veronica had always been close by when making the mold, he was somewhat out of sorts; now he knew why.

Eckhardt strolled in carrying a stack of papers and had the goggles draped over his shoulder.

"Take a look at these," Eckhardt said as he tossed the papers down onto the table.

"I printed these images that I collected with the Quantum Analyzer. They show some temporal anomalies," Eck said.

He was met with a collection of blank stares.

"The funny-looking goggles are the Quantum Analyzer," he clarified.

Everyone nodded.

"Anyway," Eckhardt leaned over the pictures, sorting through the pile. He laid three images out side by side and pushed the remainder out of the way. "Here is Möbius as he first appeared."

The image of the entity looked even more bizarre and surreal than they had remembered. Everything had happened so quickly and would take some time to process.

"I didn't remember the tentacles being so long," Veronica commented as she stared at the print. "I think I was focused on the eyes. That thing is bizarre."

Eckhardt had captured an image of Möbius in the pose of an ancient Greek philosopher posing for a statue, both arms outstretched with his hands open and palms facing the sky.

The pyramid was frozen in the image, giving everyone a nearly full view of one of the eyes. The eye seemed to stare out directly at each of them; it was eerie and disconcerting.

"Organic eyes within a pyramid of some material. Where are the blood vessels? Where are the nerves? This thing can't be alive; it must be a robot," Isaiah-Jung said.

"It looks like a collection of several systems," Eckhardt jumped in. "Look in this second image, where Möbius is preparing to leave." He pointed to an area on the next print.

The image of Möbius was starting to blur, but the rest of the scene was very clear. It was almost as if the opacity of the creature was diminishing, as if he was slightly more transparent than in the first image.

"Now, here..." Eckhardt pulled another print into the center. "Keep in mind several seconds have elapsed in between these images."

In the current image, all of the long, writhing tentacles were clustered together. The upper torso, the metal cage housing the clear ovoid shape and the pyramid, was almost horizontal now and moving back toward the horizon.

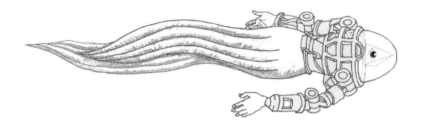

The overall image was like that of a squid fleeing from a swimmer who had come too close.

"Look at this spot behind Möbius, obviously where he's heading in this image." Eckhardt tapped a dark spot on the picture.

"I enlarged this as much as I could before it became too difficult to see," Eck said as he shuffled through the pile again.

Dark smudges dominated the image with a field of blue in the upper left corner. "This is part of the glass egg shape here," he pointed to the green field, "but look at this. This is really strange."

With some sort of reference now, each member tried to gain some perspective.

"It looks like a hole in the sky," Veronica said.

Indeed, it was as if the familiar scenery behind Möbius had been a canvas painting and someone had carelessly torn a hole in the fabric of the still life, revealing something dark and amorphous behind it.

"I believe this is a wormhole," Eckhardt said.

"So Möbius can travel in time," Sören said.

"Or at least to another dimension in the same time," he said, squinting at the dark area he thought was the beginning of the wormhole.

"Can we see beyond that opening in any of these pictures?" Sasha asked.

"Unfortunately, the next images are of the sky and then of the lens covered in canvas as I went flying through the air and destroyed the tent."

A commotion from outside distracted him from the Artifex. Pax stepped outside to see Dhaal staggering toward him carrying what looked like a piece of armor. Pax scanned the horizon for Agathi.

Dhaal came up to Pax and paused with one hand on the young man's shoulder, out of breath. Gasping, he looked up at Pax. "No time." The older man ran out of breath again. He pointed at a glowing dial on the armor breastplate that he held in his other hand.

"No time to explain," Dhaal finally got out.

With that, Dhaal grabbed the Artifex from Pax's hand, took a step back, and struck the cuirass. Before Pax could react to what was happening, Dhaal faded from view within a cocoon of violet, and then there was nothing. Pax swept his arm through the space where Dhaal had stood. If the Artifex had not disappeared, he would have sworn he was delirious. But as Pax stared into his empty palm, he realized that the Artifex Temporis was indeed gone.

CHAPTER EIGHT
(Enter the Chronomicon)

Agathi was running as fast as she could, with no sign of pursuit by the giant robotic soldiers. She was in fantastic physical condition and a seasoned runner; she was really pushing herself, and yet still felt abnormally strong and relaxed— she wasn't even breathing hard. Agathi was surprised that she could further increase her pace until she was at a constant, driving sprint. Only at that level of exertion did her heart rate finally ratchet up and faint twinges of pain flare up in her side. Even then, she felt as if she had sprouted invisible wings that were carrying her over the ground's surface.

Checking over her shoulder to insure that she was still not being followed, Agathi decided it was safe to pause for a moment and reassess her situation. It was at that point she realized how remarkably fast she had actually been moving; she could no longer see the point from which she had started running only minutes before.

She stood far out on an empty plain, devoid of any natural flora. The surface of the land felt like packed sand without any distinguishing marks. Mountains were dimly visible far away from where she stood, and she felt a sense of déjà vu, as if she had stood in this place before. However alien and lifeless the terrain appeared, something seemed familiar.

Off to her right in the distance, but not as far away as the mountain range beyond, Agathi could make out a dark cluster of jagged rock spires surrounding the base of a tower arising from the floor of the plain. Sinister in appearance, the tower had a needlelike quality and appeared of enormous height. Agathi strained to see it in its entirety, as the upper regions faded into the dimness. This was the only deviation in the otherwise barren surface in any direction, with the exception of the soldiers behind her, and offered the only potential hiding place between her and the mountain range. So she inhaled deeply and began moving toward the rocks.

A flash of light to her left hurt her eyes. For a split second, she expected one of the giants to appear beside her as they had when they captured her earlier. A heavy mass hit her from behind, and she fell to the ground. Scrambling wildly to gain her footing, she was relieved to see that it was not one of the armored giants, but Dhaal. Her fear and growing exhaustion was temporarily replaced with joy, and she threw her arms around the old man as he stood up. As Agathi held him tightly, to the point of making it difficult for Dhaal to breathe, tears welled up in her eyes. It was only with Dhaal there with her now that she could admit how terrified she had been being alone in a dark, dreary, and foreign place.

"I'm so glad to see you," she choked out, wiping the tears from her eyes as she finally released her bear hug on the elderly man. Dhaal realized how afraid she had been and how brave this young girl truly was.

"I told you I would return," he said, dusting himself off. "I thought it would be harder to find you, though."

"Did you see Pax and the others?" Agathi inquired.

"Just briefly," Dhaal replied, "just long enough to get this." Dhaal held up the Artifex Temporis.

Agathi gasped. "I'm shocked Pax gave that to you," she said.

"Well," Dhaal started, "He didn't exactly give it to me; I had to take it."

"Why?" Agathi stopped and stared at Dhaal.

"While I wasn't exactly sure how to use it, I felt it would be my only hope to find you once I returned. I thought I could reverse the passage of time, and find you with the robots, or move back even further before they captured us," Dhaal explained, "I didn't know what else to do. I didn't plan on keeping it."

"I hope not having that doesn't put Pax in trouble," Agathi said, "but I do appreciate your thinking of me."

"I didn't even have a chance to explain to Pax what I was doing. I hope he will understand," Dhaal said quietly. "I should return as soon as possible."

"We'd better keep moving for now," Agathi said. "Are you okay to walk?"

"We may not need to walk. We can use this to return home." Dhaal held up the cuirass. "I believe this is how the robots brought us here; this is how I escaped earlier and then returned just now."

He noticed that the gauge had gone dim, but went ahead and moved the needle back into the lighter area, linked arms with Agathi, and depressed the dial.

Nothing happened.

Desperate, Dhaal moved the needle back into the dark region and pressed the dial down again..

Nothing.

Dhaal panicked momentarily but sought to remain calm for Agathi's benefit. He hoped that the power would return as it had before.

"We should have returned," Dhaal told Agathi. "The gauge was glowing earlier and now it's dim. Maybe it will recharge in a few minutes."

"Let's hope so. We'll have to keep a close eye on that dial. For now, we should move on and find a place to hide. We're completely exposed out here."

"Lead the way."

The pair moved toward the outcropping at a much slower pace than before. As they neared the spires, Agathi grasped that the tower was significantly taller than she had estimated, threatening to pierce the upper regions of the atmosphere. Dhaal moved slowly but was able to maintain a steady pace.

At one point, Dhaal indicated that he needed to rest.

"No problem, Dhaal," Agathi said. "Why don't you rest here? I don't see any sign of the robots coming behind us, but let me just trot back a little ways to make sure."

"Be careful," Dhaal said as he knelt down onto the ground.

Agathi jogged back in the direction they had come, keeping her eyes peeled on the distant horizon. After a distance she gauged as reasonable, she turned back toward Dhaal.

As she reached Dhaal, he stood with his mouth agape.

Agathi panicked and turned back, expecting to see a horde of robots approaching.

She saw nothing.

"What's wrong?" she queried Dhaal.

"That was unbelievable," he started. "You moved so fast, you were a blur. You ran completely out of my sight and back in about ten seconds."

"I did notice a peculiar sense of being able to run very fast without much effort; maybe it has something to do with this place. Can time actually *behave* differently in different areas?"

"I had been thinking that it has something to do with our moving back and forth with this strange device," Dhaal said, holding up the cuirass.

"I felt a sense of strength that I had not felt in years," he continued. "When I struck him, or *it*, I should say, with my walking staff, I felt … well, I felt powerful," he said, shrugging his shoulders.

"At first, I thought it was adrenalin, but I hit that robot hard. Very hard, as we saw," Dhaal said.

Agathi thought back about the robot coming undone before them and nodded.

"You might be right," Agathi whispered. "But regardless, we need to keep moving. Although I didn't see them, I'm sure they're on their way. Who knows, they might be using those to travel out to look for us." She pointed at the copper breastplate, the gauge still so faint that it was barely visible.

The pair turned and continued onward. Eventually, they arrived without incident or any sign of the soldiers in pursuit.

Dark spires of jagged rock stood at the edge of a tor that loomed over Dhaal. Each jagged titan rose high into the sky, much taller than Agathi had originally guessed. These columns were over thirty meters tall and definitely not naturally occurring in this formation; they had been arranged by someone. Cresting the small hill, Agathi immediately knew by whom.

These spires encircled a massive depression in the ground, a near-perfect circle that spanned hundreds of meters across and descended about half of that distance. It was not a hill at all but what appeared to be a caldera. The jagged rocks sat at intervals of ten or so steps apart for the entire perimeter, creating a forbidding barrier protecting the area. Now, being this close, Agathi and Dhaal could see that every other spire was in fact a statue—two statues actually, standing back-to-back, one facing inward toward the center and one facing outward. The inner-facing statue was in a position of reverence, with the head bowed, eyes closed, and hands clasped in supplication. The opposing statue was a fearsome chimera with the sculpted and muscular body of a man and the head of an eagle. The eagle head gazed outward in a fixed, vigilant stare carved in stone. Each of these impressive guardians donned armor and clutched a massive scimitar, clearly poised in a defensive posture. Even though terrified of the situation, Agathi marveled at the scale and detail of these carvings, wondering how long they had stood here, frozen in these stances.

The floor of the entire depression was completely enshrouded in fog or steam. As the mist ebbed and flowed slowly, Agathi could that there was a layer of enormous, uniform, clear panels just beneath the surface of the steam, radiating around the floor like petals of a faded flower. Hints of shapes beneath these panels taunted Agathi's imagination; smaller dark shapes also stretched toward the center. Staring into the shifting, gray gossamer was similar to walking through a snowstorm; eventually your eyes lost their focus and you could not be sure of what you saw and what your mind imagined.

Following the direction of these real or imaginary shapes toward the distant center, Agathi gasped. A large helix of mist briefly separated, revealing Möbius in the center.

Agathi grabbed Dhaal's arm and pulled him behind one of the spires. Sharp splinters of glasslike obsidian tore at Agathi's bare arms as she slid across the surface.

"Möbius is here," she whispered.

The creature was a ridiculous distance away, but Agathi did not want to underestimate his senses and risk detection by speaking too loudly. She pulled her pack from her back and rifled through it, emerging with a set of field glasses. Peering around the edge and focusing the binoculars, Möbius came clearly into view. The pyramid within the clear ovoid was still now, and the eyes closed. A long silver conic shape shielded the tentacles, extending down over three times Möbius's body length. The sharp tip of the cone hovered above the floor of the circular plain.

Dhaal took a turn with the binoculars and stared silently for some time.

"Fascinating," was all he said, returning the field glasses to Agathi.

Just as she reached to take the glasses from Dhaal, Agathi was suddenly upended and disappeared behind the pillar. Dhaal stepped around the opposite side to see one of the giants suspending Agathi out over the edge of the canyon by her ankle. Dhaal had no question about the intention of the soldier that held her dangling.

He thought of the Artifex Temporis. Uncertain about what would happen, and upset with himself that he had not already tested out his theory, he realized he had no choice. He felt in is soul and hoped with all of his heart that this would work as he expected.

Dhaal reached into his pocket and removed the Artifex. He loosened the textured crown as gently as he could under the circumstances, but his fingers felt like clumsy sausages, and he fumbled with the device. He cursed himself and focused on remaining calm. The crown loosened, and he gently pulled up on the crown until he felt a click. He then turned the crown until he saw the red hand move backward just the slightest amount, barely noticeable. Uttering a silent prayer, he stepped back around the flint column just in time to see the giant release Agathi, dropping her into the gorge.

Dhaal depressed the crown and heard it click into place.

It was as if he were dropped into a vat of warm molasses. This was the first vivid sensation that he had experienced since he had returned to this place, wherever it was. Warmth covered him, and he initially panicked, feeling the sensation of drowning. Dhaal calmed somewhat as he realized he was not actually immersed in fluid but that this was some effect on his nervous system; he could breathe normally, with just a slight sensation of pressure on his chest. A strange thought passed through his mind that this must be the sensation of being a fish, submerged but able to breathe. His eyesight was very fuzzy, and as numbness began to spread through his body, everything grew darker. Normally, Dhaal thought these would be the sensations associated with catastrophic events, such as a heart attack or a stroke. But he sensed that this was not the case and found himself relaxing and without fear. As quickly as the numbness spread, it began to diminish and was replaced by a tingling sensation that started at his fingertips and spread inward. His vision was returning, and he was starting to vaguely identify shapes around him. He wanted to call out to Agathi, but his voice would not yet respond. Agathi finally came into view off to his left, and he began to unconsciously twist his torso in that direction. Dhaal felt like a ship moving through icy waters; he could see where he wanted to go, but it was difficult to maneuver to that point. All of these strange sensations quickly faded.

Dhaal was staring at Agathi, who stood with her arm outstretched to take the field glasses from him.

I didn't turn the dial far enough back! Dhaal thought. Dropping the binoculars, he grabbed his walking staff and quickly moved around the stone pillar. He rounded the opposite side just as the soldier was beginning to crouch down and reach around toward Agathi. Taking advantage of the robot's awkward stance and his own forward momentum, Dhaal jammed his walking stick into the ground at the base of the column and leveraged the robot over the edge of the cliff before it could adjust its center of gravity or grab at Agathi's ankle.

The giant lurched forward trying to regain its balance while reaching back for Dhaal at the same time, failing on both counts. Dhaal and Agathi watched the soldier careen over the edge and into the pit. They could clearly see the soldier's face before it dropped below the rim of the canyon; there was no expression whatsoever. Just because it was so human in appearance, Dhaal had expected a scream when the being went over the edge, and the silence that followed was both unnerving and bizarre.

As the machine fell, it finally began to emit a piercing and shrill signal, electronic in nature. A cutting white beam of light shot outward from the robot's eyes, directed at the center of the circle, where the dormant Möbius hovered.

Dhaal continued around the jagged rock pillar to check on Agathi, who was moving around the opposite side to look for him. They crashed headlong into each other.

"Dhaal, how did you know the soldier was there? You moved so quickly!"

"I'll explain later. I think we're in trouble," he said, turning back toward Möbius.

"Who dare enter the Chronomicon?"

The voice was terrifying and thunderous, echoing throughout the circular valley.

"I think you're right," Agathi responded.

Dhaal looked through the field glasses once again. The eyes were now open, and the pyramidal structure was beginning to spin. He saw a wave of lights beginning to touch the tops of the rocks that covered the floor of the canyon, starting close by Möbius and radiating outward.

"Those dark shapes in the mist are more soldiers!" Agathi yelled. "They're animating!"

A wave of fear gripped the two as they watched the activity unfold across the sea of automatons below. The number of these dopplegängers was staggering; Dhaal could not imagine the havoc and destruction such a force could wreak. There were thousands of these monsters stirring into action at the call of their master.

Dhaal looked down at the corselet; the gauge now glowed brightly. Dhaal took Agathi's hand and drove his elbow firmly down onto the glowing gauge. Too late, Dhaal realized he had not altered the setting on the dial. Dhaal and Agathi found themselves thrown out onto the plain, just a matter of meters away from where they had just stood. Rolling over the surface of the ground in a flurry of dust, Dhaal clung fiercely onto the cuirass. Coming to a stop in a heap, he first checked to make sure Agathi was okay. Her youthful strength and agility allowed her to remain on her feet while being hurled through space. Dhaal then glanced down at the piece of armor that served as their escape mechanism, hoping to see the light still glowing brightly. In disappointment, the gauge was completely dim. He had wasted the charge they needed to return home and would have to wait.

Although the breastplate device had not served the purpose Dhaal had intended, it had moved them out of view of the army of mechanical hominids that currently stirred to action below. Dhaal thought of the Artifex but was too unsure of its effect. He did not want to move backward in time to once again be captured by the robots, or forward into the unknown. He and Agathi would rely on their own resourcefulness for survival.

As the waves of soldiers below turned toward Dhaal and Agathi, their malevolent, glowing eyes met empty space.

CHAPTER NINE
(An evil genius awakens)

"Bonaventure? How do you feel?" Goethe said quietly with the inflection of one speaking to a small child.

Dr. Goethe stood before one of the transport ships and it felt bizarre trying to initiate a conversation with a spacecraft.

"Bonaventure. Can you hear me?"

"Of course I can hear you, Jonas," replied a heavily synthesized voice. "Can you hear me is a better question? Speaking is such a strange sensation without vocal chords or a mouth. It is difficult to distinguish between speaking and thinking."

A wave of relief swept over Dr. Goethe as he realized the surgery had been a success. A supreme sense of accomplishment filled his being, just as when he had performed the first human-to-human brain transplant years before. Except with this experiment there was also a sub-current of dread intertwined with the elation of his accomplishment, a distinct and foreboding sense of impending catastrophe.

"Yes, Bonaventure, I can hear you."

"Congratulations, Jonas. You obviously did well.

"My vital signs look good, you might increase the level of serotonin, and I believe you can eliminate the drip of antibiotics into the Somatic Kernel's synthetic cranium. Also, please adjust the attack rate on the vocal synthesizer," Golding instructed.

Dr. Goethe scanned the array of varied monitors searching through the results. The sense of dread ratcheted up in his gut as his mind raced to understand how Golding was reaching these conclusions. Could he actually see the monitors? He had not yet made the connections between the optical nerve and the visual junction center.

Dr. Goethe moved toward the base of the ship, where the cylinder that now housed Dr. Bonaventure Golding's brain was mounted into the chassis. The arrangement of the area within the hull was definitely different since he had last checked. The differences were subtle, but things had definitely been altered within the clear capsule.

"Annuit Coeptus," said Golding.

"What?" Goethe shot back.

"The eye of Providence looks favorably upon our venture."

Goethe ignored him; he was not interested in Golding's paraphrasing of Virgil at the moment.

"Have you informed the committee that I ... that SomKern5 is ready for the launch?" Dr. Golding asked.

"Bonaventure, this is the first moment you've been conscious. Do you think I can just call up the committee and say, 'Hi, everyone, this is Dr. Goethe. Although the surgery was just performed a few weeks ago, and I have absolutely no test results, I can guarantee you that SomKern5 is absolutely ready to go!'"

"I don't see why not, Jonas. I told you I feel fine. And I have been conscious since almost immediately after the surgery. This is just the first moment that you're aware that I am conscious." Golding's synthetic voice was very strong, and unbelievably, actually had a more pleasant tone than his natural speaking voice.

Studying the contents of the capsule, he finally identified that a pair of the external manipulator digits, mechanical hands actually, were now inside the capsule. This seemed impossible. Dr. Goethe was growing confused. No one should be able to access the interior of the ship, not even him. Golding had successfully transitioned the brain into this special chamber nearly a week ago. Today was the first sign of any response. Goethe had seen the cerebral activity on a sharp increase since late last night and had been vigilant in monitoring Bonaventure for further activity ever since.

"Bonaventure," Goethe asked gently. "Have you made changes to the structure of the ship?"

"Yes, Jonas. Beginning almost the first day, when the entire system was in sterile isolation after the surgery. I took advantage of the isolation and darkness to make improvements. I started with the optical sensors; there really is no need to wait on making those connections, Jonas, and they were quite simple. There are still quite a number of things that need to be corrected or improved."

Goethe's mind raced, trying to figure out exactly how Golding could actually do anything. The design was such that the Somatic Kernel could control the ship only once in flight. The monitors should have indicated the slightest amount of activity in Golding's brain, triggering all manner of alarms and indicators to catch Goethe's attention. Golding must have somehow intervened and blocked the sensors from displaying any activity.

The fear ratcheted up another notch as he imagined what other sorts of changes Golding could have made during this period when Goethe thought him completely inactive.

"I noticed the robotic hands are inside the capsule, Bonaventure. Did you make that modification?"

Dr. Goethe knew the answer but hoped his rhetorical question would distract Bonaventure as he began to walk around the hull of the ship, moving toward an emergency disconnect that he had installed. There was always a fear that things could go horribly awry when bringing a Somatic Kernel on-line. Goethe had experienced a great deal of anxiety considering what could happen when a brain with Golding's intelligence, a genius among geniuses, regained consciousness. The disconnect switch would disable the Somatic Kernel completely and return manual control.

"Don't bother, Jonas. I removed the failsafe. There was really no need to have that in place. Someone could accidentally disable my function; it was far too dangerous."

Goethe froze in his tracks. Swallowing hard, he tried to speak in a normal tone.

"That was just in case of emergency, Bonaventure. It was really more to protect you than anything else," Goethe lied. "That could have made it easy to transport you into another Somatic Kernel unit."

His voice sounded weak and desperate. Beads of sweat erupted on his brow.

"I'm sure it was, Jonas. Why are you so nervous?"

Goethe made a break and ran for the double doors at the end of the lab that led into a transitional clean room. As he pushed through the first set of doors, he heard the magnetic locks on the outer doors engage and knew he was trapped.

There were no windows on the outer doors as there were on the inner, and he knew it would be futile to pound on the doors and yell for help; this entire section of this facility was designed for absolute silence for the recovering Somatic Kernels. From an intercom speaker mounted in the ceiling, he heard Golding speak, "I think you need to make the call and confirm that Bonaventure Golding III, this ship, is ready for launch tomorrow, Jonas," Golding said very flatly.

"I won't do it," he replied with a mixture of fear and anger.

"You already did, Jonas."

A loud dial tone blared from a phone console just on the other side of the inner doors, and Goethe almost jumped from his lab coat. He saw the LED indicating an open line begin to blink a deep blue. The small light seemed like an emergency siren in his mind, but he knew there was no one to see the beacon of danger.

The melodic tones of a number being dialed on a digital phone filled the air.

"Launch committee headquarters," a voice stated matter-of-factly.

"This is Dr. Jonas Goethe," his own voice announced.

He was confused at first, but then thought back to his conversation only moments ago with Golding, where he had sarcastically mocked Bonaventure's question. Golding had obviously been recording their conversation and was playing back selected excerpts.

Had Golding actually lured him into that conversation? His fear notched up again, considering how easily he had been manipulated by this superior rogue intelligence.

"Hello, Dr. Goethe. What's the status of SomKern5?"

"I can guarantee you that SomKern5 is absolutely ready to go!"

Goethe heard his voice again and slammed at the releases of the inner doors, but to no avail.

"Great news! I was expecting this after we heard from Dr. Golding earlier. He was very disappointed that he had to leave the country this afternoon and wouldn't be present at the launch but was very pleased with the progress of the system."

Bonaventure has been a busy boy, Goethe thought. He now regretted that Golding had talked him into performing the surgery and that he had insisted on anonymity. No one knew that Bonaventure Golding had been the source of the brain for this Somatic Kernel, and he had covered his tracks well by creating an alibi that had him conveniently leaving the country,

"We'll list SomKern5 as the primary command in the series. We'll move the capsule to the launch site staging area tonight. We need to load up some cephalopod specimens—big ones."

"Congratulations!" was the last thing Goethe heard before the light blinked out. He imagined his own lights would be extinguished shortly as well.

CHAPTER TEN
(Sasha Platamone Liesel von Weimar)

Sasha Platamone Liesel von Weimar was the product of a father from the northern area of the Teutonic State and a mother from the Hellenic Island State. Her family was of vague renown in her mother's country because her grandfather had actually assisted in engineering the canal that created the Island State, cleaving it from the mainland of the Pan-European landmass almost two decades ago.

Sasha sat on the floor in her library, surrounded by stacks of books. It was a fairly routine occurrence to find Sasha here engulfed in some piece of literature or scouring some fact-filled tome.

Her mother called in the distance, but Sasha did not hear her. With a name like Sasha's, her mother did not ever use her full name, even when she was very upset with Sasha. Sasha always joked that by the time her mother recited her whole name, that she would have forgotten what had upset her in the first place!

Sasha loved books and fondly remembered the day that she and Pax had discovered the wing of a library, still intact after so many years. A group of people from the village had been on one of the periodic treks to scour the landscape where the ruins from the Ecology War had been buried and marked off-limits until the radiation had dissipated. After excavating no deeper than her knees, Sasha's pickaxe had struck a large plastic panel. After clearing the soil away by hand, a spotlight had revealed a large room filled with books. The environment within the underground chamber had fortunately remained optimal to keep the books in perfect condition.

Finder's rights had given Sasha the right of first refusal on the library, and she took her time deciding what she wanted to keep for herself and what she wanted to donate to the small public library in Orneth.

Several days of hauling books back and forth between her parents' home and the excavation site on an oxcart had yielded hundreds of books and enough beautiful mahogany shelves to shelve all of her newfound treasure three times over, as well as all of the books that she had collected before. Her father's reluctant agreement to let her use a decent-sized portion of their barn created a wonderful escape and haven of learning for Sasha.

Sasha's father had come from a long line of skilled woodworkers. In the evenings that followed after Sasha had dragged all of her treasures to the barn, he had assembled the bookshelves, modifying each one so that the highest shelf of each bookcase was within Sasha's reach. With the remaining wood, he built her a long reading table with a wonderfully solid bench on either side.

She moved to that table now. A kerosene lantern burned brightly among stacks of books patiently waiting, either to be returned to their cozy resting spot on the shelves or to be skimmed through again. The warmth of the lantern was welcomed and familiar. Tonight, the lantern was helping to keep Sasha's hands warm as the chill of evening slowly crept into the barn to join her.

Veronica's earlier comment about a hole in the sky had triggered a thought, and Sasha now pored through a series of volumes dedicated to space and time, searching for a treatise she had read in the not too distant past. It was a beautiful set of books bound in deep burgundy leather, an encyclopedia of all information available at the time it had been written. She knew it involved a collection of facts as well as many theories discussing parallel dimensions, and she thought it would be of interest to browse through the broad spectrum of theories. Based on the creature's ramblings, everyone was assuming that Möbius was truly moving through time. But from something she had read, Sasha had a hunch that Möbius was actually moving between two or more parallel dimensions.

Neither of these phenomenon was a simple feat, and both pushed the envelope of her understanding, but Sasha felt that this fine distinction between time travel and movement between parallel dimensions might play an important role in their ability to fight Möbius.

She had read this prior to the appearance of Möbius, and while very interesting from a theoretical perspective, at that time it had not held the immediate relevance that it now possibly could.

Thumbing through the large volume, starting at the back (a habit that Sasha had developed as a child, one which drove the librarian at her elementary school absolutely insane and made Sasha all the more grateful for having her own library now), moving from the last section about ionic radiation toward "Continuum, Time–Space," she froze. Taking up half of a page in the deep space colonization chapter was the image that had haunted her since she had seen Möbius appear. She had not been able to completely recall this image or make a strong association until now.

Sasha placed a bright red bookmark on the page and loudly slammed the volume shut. She would show this to Eckhardt later.

Just as the book closed, her mother rounded the end of the bookcase.

"Pax and several of your friends are here to see you," she said.

"Is Agathi with them?" Sasha asked anxiously. She was growing sick with worry that Agathi had not yet returned.

"I didn't see her. Dinner's almost ready. Why don't you have everyone stay and eat?"

Sasha agreed. She knew that Pax wanted to go over their plans one more time since tomorrow was the day that Möbius said to bring the Artifex Temporis to him. She also guessed (correctly) that they were all hoping for dinner here anyway. It was, after all, important to eat, especially when trying to figure out how to save the world.

CHAPTER ELEVEN
(Möbius returns)

Loud explosions riddled the air. All of the OCL members had been in position since before sunrise and as ready as they could be to face Möbius, unsure of exactly what to expect. They had trained a great deal but only partially tested their abilities under pressure, and they had definitely never prepared for a robotic, squid-like alien that traveled through multiple dimensions.

Once several years before, the newly formed Order of the Celestial Lotus had received word that a group of roving bandits had been on a crime spree and were traveling north on the roadway toward Orneth. The tales of the bandits' actions had of course been wildly exaggerated to the point that the legendary Attila the Hun would have been more welcome into Orneth than the approaching group. So the Order had decided to take action and formulated a plan.

Pax thought back to their experience with the thugs from many years ago, and recalled the gang leader's telling of their encounter.

Morning sunlight glistened on the dew-covered leaves that hid Slake, Kleider, and seven other less-than-reputable of their colleagues. The dense green foliage of these low bushes provided the perfect hiding place for seeing the unsuspecting oxcarts approaching down this section of the road as it straightened before descending into the village of Orneth.

Slake was the leader of the band if there was one. He was by far the most educated, and the only one of the crew that could think more than a few steps ahead. His real name was Winnifer Slayton Goodberry, but he thought revealing that would certainly put an end to his rule as gang leader, so had opted for the rougher sounding Slake. (This idea had come from a female traveler whose load he had just lightened vis-à-vis her jewelry. She had called him a snake. Between her heavy accent and nervous anxiety, it had come out "Slake," and Winnifer Slayton Goodberry had immediately ceased to exist.)

Tall and thin with an aquiline nose, dark eyes, and thinning hair, he kept a leather hat with a wide brim on to keep his head warm and cover his balding pate. The hat was made with inferior materials: swatches of improperly tanned leather sewn onto strips of what appeared to be pig skin, complete with clumps of pig hair still clinging to the sickly gray hide. Not a single panel of the hat matched in color.

All in all, it seemed to suit Slake's character perfectly.

He was wrapped in a threadbare blanket that reeked of sweat and fish entrails. Kleider was his right-hand man, but Slake knew that he could no more trust Kleider than he could trust a rat. Kleider was a heavier-set, muscular man with a thick jaw and a heavy brow that jutted out so far you could barely see that he even had eyes. A thick black shadow of a beard started just below his hidden eyes and disappeared into the neckline of a stained canvas jacket.

This rag-tag group had been on the run for several days after a succession of heists and petty thefts in villages and camps all along the roadways.

Water collected on the leaves and dripped down onto the men, further soaking their filthy clothes and reminding them of how cool the morning was. This was as close to a bath as most of this motley crew had seen in weeks, if not longer. No one had been by for hours, and they were getting edgy, about ready to give up hope for the rest of the day.

As the sun climbed higher into the sky, the waiting group heard the familiar sound of iron-rimmed wooden wheels, heavy with a load, approaching. These travelers were coming from Orneth, and Slake hoped that they had done a lot of shopping in the village and that they carried plenty of extra money, as well. The thieves had collected quite a bit of booty over the past several weeks, and he knew that it was time to lay low for a while. But the approaching winter and the greed that swelled from their recent successes pushed him to keep working for at least a few more days. He hoped they would have enough loot to support them like kings over the bitter, cold season ahead. Last year had not been so successful, and this past winter had been miserable. Slake unconsciously flexed his left hand, feeling the burn in his joints from his arthritis, and he shivered thinking back to how much his hand had hurt from sleeping out in the elements.

News would have traveled of their activities, but he hoped that they had pushed hard enough to stay a day or so ahead of any warnings. The sweat under the saddles of the nearby horses they had stolen several days back was a testament to how hard they had ridden in the last twelve hours. The poor animals were overloaded with sacks, bags, and boxes of stolen goods.

The sound of the cart grew louder. Kleider peered down the road to catch a glimpse of their approaching prize. He whispered to Slake that it was a covered wagon and that the animal pulling the cart had to work hard to carry their loot up the hill. He smiled a near toothless smile. Wet strands of hair were pasted onto his large and cadaverous forehead.

Slake imagined himself being carted down the road, comfortably lounging inside a covered oxcart, sprawling on a bed of valuable pelts, not the lice-ridden kind with tufts of hair missing like he had stashed in his pack. He envisioned eating meats and vegetables in the warm glow of a kerosene lantern, listening to recorded music as the winter snows fell outside. None of these things was he willing to work for, beyond the effort involved in stealing them from someone who had worked hard to obtain them.

He leaned back and signaled to the others across the road to be prepared. The pistol he carried was an old revolver, pitted with spots of rust along the barrel. One of the pearl handles was loose and had a dark crack spreading outward from the screws that had once held it secure. Even with these scars of age and neglect, it was still an advanced and superior weapon when compared against the crossbow, axe, mace, and pitchforks held by the others. Being the leader of this group had its privileges when it came to selecting the best weapons from their heists. He checked that the chambers of the revolver were full and that he had extra bullets on the ammo belt. This pistol was probably older than he was, but it was new to him as of two days ago, and he had not yet had to actually discharge it. So far, waving it menacingly had accomplished everything he needed.

He made a few hand signals, reminding them of the strategy they had mapped out earlier based on the lay of the land. A lookout was stationed farther down the road in both directions to watch for the approach of lawmen while they conducted their business with the owners of this cart.

As the oxcart was almost upon them, Slake gave the signal, and the robbers sprang from their hiding places. Slake and Kleider jumped in front of the cart, flailing their arms, Slake holding the pistol and Kleider waving a sword.

It was a young couple driving the cart, not more than fifteen years old or so. Golden hair fell from within a scarf the young woman wore over her head, flowing out into a liquid frame around her stunning turquoise eyes. The young man was broad—chested with a slender face and sandy blonde hair.

The man the gang referred to as Muth walked over and laughed. "Doesn't get much easier than this," he chuckled, "I almost feel guilty taking these kids' belongings without even a fair fight."

"But I'll bet you still sleep like a baby tonight, Muth, under their blankets, after eating their food!" another man yelled out. The whole gang roared with laughter.

"Let's see what we have in here," Kleider said as he walked around the back of the cart and flung open the canvas panels. No sooner had he poked his head in to look than he went sailing out from the wagon, landing flat on his back on the ground.

Before anyone realized what was happening, a stream of darkly clad figures appeared from inside the cart. Completely covered in armor, the likes of such these bandits had never seen, these dark, masked figures quickly moved to surround the robbers that stood dumbfounded.

Slake fumbled for his gun and raised it toward the closest armored figure. As he moved his thumb to cock the pistol, a blunt-tipped arrow came from nowhere and struck the back of his hand. The gun dropped to the ground, and excruciating pain shot up through is arm and into his shoulder. Slake looked at his throbbing hand and immediately knew that, at the very least, several bones were shattered. A large black bruise was already spreading across his swelling red hand. A wave of nausea washed over him, and he crumpled to his knees. Slake looked up and saw a beautiful young woman with flowing red hair walking toward him. She carried a bow and had already reloaded a fresh arrow. This arrow did not have a blunt tip. The sun glinted off of the razor sharp edges of an arrow obviously designed for hunting large game—much larger game than Slake.

As he kept his eyes on the approaching girl, he could see in his peripheral vision that his companions were being dealt with quite readily by these mysterious vigilantes. The young couple that had been driving the oxcart had shed their country garb, which had masked protective armor beneath, and had joined their companions in subduing the rest of Slake's crew. He saw his lookout on the road in the distance, running away from the scene in fear, leaving them to fend for themselves. Such was the character of the companions he had chosen.

A set of strong, gloved hands grabbed him from behind and lifted him to his feet. With a less-than-gentle motion, he was moved into a line with the other captive and incapacitated members of his group.

Slake stared at the ground, waiting for the worst to come. A pair of heavily plated boots came into his vision. He lifted his eyes and was face-to-face with a fearsome mask, cast of bronze. A permanent grimace of loathing and disgust was formed into the hard countenance that faced him. Sparkles glimmered from the eyes recessed behind the empty carved sockets of the mask.

The voice of a young man surprisingly rang out, "You will have the chance to repay your debt to society through honest, hard work. You will begin by returning everything you have taken to the rightful owners."

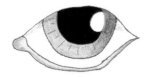

That had been Pax's voice from within the samurai mask. He never tired of remembering that story, or hearing one of the Order repeat it. Although years had passed, he clearly recalled the pride he felt when he ordered the bandits to be moved into the cart. Unquestionably defeated, the ragged band of thugs had complied quickly, eager to be out of the presence of these unexpected enforcers of the law.

Once they had returned to Orneth and made arrangements for the bandits to be held in one of the city buildings until work could be arranged for them, the Order of the Celestial Lotus gathered together.

"Everyone should be proud," Pax had led off. "We passed a crucial test today. I have faith in each of you and in the Order of the Celestial Lotus as a team. Our success proved we are ready."

"Here, here!" the group had joined in.

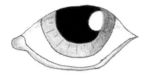

Now almost three years later, the group stood more prepared, still with faith in their abilities and each other, but having no real idea what they were to face in terms of the upcoming battle.

"At some point, someone from a long time away will try to take this from you—they must not succeed. You need to be prepared to do whatever is necessary to guard this."

Now Isolde's mysterious words made perfect sense, and their mission was crystal clear.

So much had happened in the years that passed. On one level, it was a relief that Isolde's warning of a stranger coming to regain the Artifex Temporis was finally over. On another, it was terrifying that the stranger was some bizarre being with an army of giants at its command. Now, hidden within a sheaf of hay, Pax and Eckhardt waited for their enemy to return.

Another explosion shook their hiding place. Eckhardt covered his ears to muffle the thunderous explosions. He knew these sounds heralded the arrival of Möbius or his minions and wondered how far away they were. All of the OCL were in relatively close proximity, and Eck wondered if these detonations were as deafening for them.

Hazarding detection, Eck parted the hay and peeked outside. Purple flashes and the erratic pulses of static discharge peppered the horizon. Eckhardt thought that if each of these events indicated a separate enemy arrival, just based on the limited visibility he had from within the sheaf, they were vastly outnumbered. Another blast of violet light, this one very close by, caused Eckhardt to quickly retreat into the haystack. Peeking out again, he saw a pair of giants standing in the midst of a smoldering patch of land.

His heart leapt into his throat. If these two represented Möbius's warriors, their chances were non-existent.

The twin soldiers stood immobile for some time, seemingly at military attention. Moments later, they turned away from Eck's hiding spot and stared at a point on the ridge of the nearby hill. Eckhardt sucked in his breath as he saw that spinning eye contained within the glass ovoid rising over the hilltop.

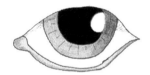

Veronica felt exposed standing, on the upper level of the windmill. Isaiah-Jung was positioned within eyesight, just above her on a catwalk that spanned the narrow space high above the ground floor where they had entered this empty structure. She stood close by a door that opened out on a deck that encircled the structure of the windmill, about fifteen meters up from the ground. She kept her back pressed against the wall, stepping in front of the door to peer through a small pane of textured glass.

Veronica was partially armored, and uncomfortable. As an archer, she felt very restricted when wearing protective gear, always feeling like her accuracy was reduced. Pax had insisted on everyone being safe, but Veronica had drawn the line at her helmet. Instead, she had compromised on a partial faceguard, which seemed to interfere a great deal less than did a full helmet. Sporting her usual ponytails, Veronica had added a series of polished brass rings to the ends of each tress in an attempt to keep them out of the way and under control when using her bow.

The windmill itself was strategically positioned within forty meters of the point that Möbius had specified that they wait for his return. Veronica could easily hit that area from this distance, barring any unforeseen high winds. She had trained by shooting from just about every position possible on the windmill, and could not even hazard a guess at how many volleys she had launched from the deck. Many hay bales, fence posts, and flour sacks had met their demise from arrows loosed from this perch high above the ground. The arrows that now filled her quiver were much heavier than the precision arrows that Veronica always crafted, and their intent was far more deadly.

She lifted one of the arrows that Eck had fashioned for her and studied it closely. The shaft of the arrow was some sort of fiber that flexed quite a bit but seemed extremely strong. The fletching was enormous relative to the traditional feather ones that Veronica used; she knew that this was to account for the significant weight and heavier tip. Where a metallic arrowhead usually attached was a long glass tube that ran almost a quarter of the length of the arrow, with a glistening syringe needle protruding ominously from the end. Eck had placed a small cork on the end of each needle for her protection as well as to keep the smoky yellow fluid contained within: a cocktail of active viruses that would have adverse effects on almost any living species, including her. The fluid completely filled this otherwise clear chamber. Eckhardt had gone to great pains to eliminate any air so as to keep the fluid from sloshing about and affecting the balance of the arrow. A silver bearing sat at the base of the cylinder where it attached to the shaft; this mass would force the contents of the tube out through the needle when it struck, hopefully injecting and infecting Möbius.

Veronica shuddered as she gently returned the arrow to the quiver.

After an explosion that sent tremors through the windmill, Veronica heard Isaiah-Jung gasp.

"He's here. Möbius is here. Get ready."

Veronica thought that the confidence in Isaiah-Jung's voice was forced for her benefit. She very much appreciated the effort.

She knocked one of the deadly arrows and took a deep breath.

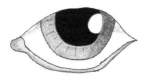

Sasha and Sören worked feverishly. Sören anxiously studied waveforms on an oscilloscope, while Sasha made adjustments to antenna assembly that she had just connected up to a router. When everything was completely connected and adjusted properly, this conglomeration of eclectic hardware and software would broadcast the malicious code with which they hoped to infect Möbius. This writhing mass of cables and bristling antennae constituted Eckhardt's viral beacon.

Sasha's jet black hair was matted with sweat from working under the intense halogen lights suspended above. She reached up, holding a smoldering soldering iron, and wiped her brow with the back of her arm. She wore magnifying glasses that made her already large, brown eyes seem huge.

Sasha was armored from the waist down, and the dark patches where perspiration soaked through the leather chemise she wore were now larger than the dry areas. Her breastplate and helmet lay close by. As had each member of the Order of the Celestial Lotus, Sasha had designed her own armor. Whereas Pax and Sören had drawn heavily from ancient Asian influences, such as samurai and the Silla Royal Guard, she had based the foundation of her design on historic Scandinavian armor, incorporating some elements of even older Mesopotamian design. Sasha's helmet was a combination of bronze and some panels of carbon fiber that she had liberated from Ecology War surplus. The helmet rose up into a point, which was graced with a large tuft of coarse black and gray animal hair. A band of shiny black fur ran across her brow and around the helmet, from which two large and polished black horns protruded outward and then curved back toward the top. Veins of white ran from the base of each horn up to the needle-sharp tips, one located above each eye. The effect was intimidating and gave the impression that she was charging forward even when she was at rest. When fully armored, she donned a veil of tightly woven chain mail that covered her face from just below her eyes and draped down to cover her neck, coming to rest on her breastplate.

"Those bursts of static electricity are wreaking havoc on our transmitter," Sören told Sasha.

Sweat also dripped from his face, and he was frustrated by the amount of time it was taking to finalize the calibration of the beacon. Each time they heard one of the sonic blasts, they would alternate to look out of the slit of a window at the very top of this small underground room in which they worked. The generator they needed to power this concoction sputtered away near the door, adding to the heat and smell; Sören had vented the exhaust outside, but the hot smell still wafted in, unwelcomed. Sören referred to this place as a bunker; Sasha had always just called it her family's root cellar.

Sasha and Sören could see the very uppermost section of the windmill tower and the slowly spinning blades. Eckhardt's hiding spot was blocked by a hillock of earth that rose up to the left of their tiny window, but they knew he was close.

With the echo from the most recent explosion still lingering in the air, Sören was peering through the window. These had been the loudest, and he estimated that their targets were nearby. Looking up to his right, he saw the upper door of the windmill open slowly and watched Veronica step out onto the deck. She left the door ajar and edged cautiously around the windmill with her bow held out before her; Sören could see that she had an arrow readied. Veronica's release of the first of Eck's giant arrows was each group's call to action.

"Veronica's ready!" he called out to Sasha. "Can we connect the antenna?"

"Almost. I just need to finish soldering this connector," Sasha called out more loudly than she had intended. She was nervous, and her right eye stung from the sweat than trickled down from her brow, but she was still able to focus on her task.

The connector she was soldering broke free and fell to the ground.

"Sören! Help!" Sasha yelled. She was panicking now and afraid that they wouldn't be finished with their part when Veronica made the first shot. No one knew which of the three attacks would affect Möbius, and they did not want to let the rest of the team down.

She had rolled into a prone position and was stretching to reach the connector. The muscles in her arms burned, but she could not reach the connector without crawling out of her current spot and jumping down to where the connector lay. Sasha did not think she could squeeze out, get the connector, and worm her way back into this claustrophobic spot in time.

"Hurry!" Sören called out. He had obviously not heard her cry.

Sasha thought quickly. Time was running out, so she just held the wire up against the fitting and covered the whole area in a mass of silver solder. Small flecks of resin sprayed out and landed on the lenses of the magnifying glasses. Sasha blinked but did not look away from her task. When she pulled the smoking soldering iron away, the connection was not pretty, but she thought it would do the job.

"Finished!" she called out and shimmied her way out of the tight space as Sören activated the beacon.

Sasha strapped on her helmet and buckled up her breastplate as she followed Sören up and out of the cellar. He carried a large pike and a club for each of them, and a small crossbow dangled from his belt.

CHAPTER TWELVE
(An unexpected enigma)

Bonaventure Golding mentally blinked his eyes. The sensation seemed real even though his optic nerves were connected to a miasma of external sensors.

The heaviness associated with deep cryogenic sleep was slow to dissipate, and Golding found himself concentrating on the date long before it truly registered. He had been in cryo-sleep for just over one hundred years.

Gigantic volumes of data poured into his awareness, and he quickly assessed that he had been awakened due to a completely unexpected occurrence in flight.

Even as he sorted through the data mentally, part of his awareness drifted off in amazement at his surroundings. At launch, Golding had been placed in cryogenic suspension, so even though he had been traveling through space for over one hundred years, this was the first time he had actually seen space. He marveled at the waves of light that danced on the surface of the inky black sea of space. Stars abounded as well as comets, nebulas, and myriad galaxies, all beautifully contrasted against the beautiful void beyond.

Almost immediately after Golding had been disembodied, or "freed from the restraints of his mortal coil" as he now thought of it, he had started suffering from delusions of grandeur, feelings of immense superiority. Golding had always felt superior to other people throughout his previous life, as well, and in no way recognized his perspective as delusional; he was quite convinced that he was indeed an exceptional creation. Just like a gas in the vacuum of space, his ego strived to fill the endless expanse.

Without the obvious effects of time on the human body, which serves as a constant reminder to most people of their mortality, Golding began to have difficulty in his perception of time. His temporal references in terms to the memories of his life seemed to have been stretched out of proportion or removed entirely. Golding began to recall his life as a research scientist as being from thousands of years ago, and his current hybrid form of part human and part robotics as having been in existence for even longer.

It was a very short jump from these false memories to the perceptions of immortality.

Golding truly felt like a god, an immortal being sailing through the depths of space that no human had ever seen directly (he thought this in terms of "no man has ever seen this with his own eyes," and commented to himself that he was not actually "seeing" this with his own eyes either but through various cameras and other sensors).

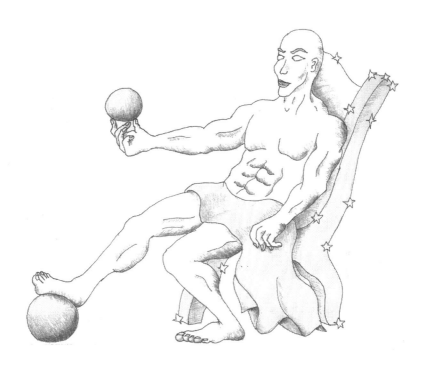

He pictured himself as an ancient Greek god, seated on a throne of stars at the center of creation, the universe circling about him. In his mental image, he had a strong and muscular physical body, poised sprawling and relaxed on a celestial dais, but at the same time, so very regal in appearance. Golding rested his foot on a large sun and carelessly spun a planet on his fingertips.

The sheer extent of the deepness of space was mind-boggling, even for intelligence such as SomKern5, née Bonaventure Golding III. A breathtaking parade of white lights and colorful gases, shades of pinks, blues, and greens previously captured only in the images of deep-space telescopes, not doing justice to the actual, graced each direction he looked.

Analyzing the images from the banks of external sensors on the ship, he quickly saw the anomaly that had most probably triggered the disturbance of his cryo-sleep. A distinct area of absolute blackness stood out against the ubiquitous points of light distributed across the fabric that engulfed him. The realization of what he was seeing produced the dual sensations of excitement and fear. He was staring into a black hole.

Wisps of light from a nearby star were converging into a gossamer thread that flowed outward in a graceful arc and then disappeared into a small, inky black hole. Stars shone brightly all around, with the exception of the anomaly that was devouring the helpless asymptotic red giant that happened to be in the wrong part of the universe at the wrong time.

Golding scanned through the data and found entries in the information that indicated the detection of this rogue presence only minutes earlier than he was awakened. This was the cause for concern detected by the automated systems on board. He searched through the pages of information to see if there had been any other entries anticipating such an encounter, only to find two related entries. One stated an insignificant statistical probability of encountering a black hole. The second entry was from a renowned astrophysicist who warned of this scenario, touting his calculations that all but guaranteed that such a black hole would interfere on the planned course to the sea planet. The astrophysicist had been overruled in the interest of a shorter path.

The automatic pilot of the ship was fighting to stay on a course that would give this destructive force a wide berth, and was doing reasonably well. Warning lights and sirens blazed throughout the ship. The effect of the crushing gravity created by the black hole was unmistakable, but the sensation was new. Applying a wide range of filters to observe the black hole, Golding found himself fascinated with the enigmatic phenomenon, amazed at the power such an entity possessed.

The fear of being in the proximity of such a destructive force was completely absent. While factual information and logic told him that his ship could be completely obliterated by the gravity within the black hole, his delusions completely dismissed such warnings as not applying to a god. He was an immortal, moving freely within the confines of his universal playground, and nothing could harm a god.

In almost a dreamlike state, Golding overrode the automatic pilot of the ship and began to manually guide the ship toward the center of the black hole, drawn to it like a moth to a flame. The sensation that an ethereal voice beckoned to him was overwhelming, and he was completely oblivious to the various alarms and warning signs that erupted all about him as the ship plunged into the heart of this incomprehensibly powerful blackness.

CHAPTER THIRTEEN
(Möbius comes to collect)

Möbius stood on top of a hill surrounded by at least twenty of the giant soldiers. When Möbius first appeared only seven days ago, he had floated mysteriously in the air. This led everyone to speculate hopefully that the Möbius was either the product of mass hysteria or some sort of illusion consisting only of sight and sound but no real substance. Veronica had thought Möbius a nightmare, an unreal specter produced by her psyche to represent some unknown disturbance elsewhere in her life. Learning that everyone shared the same experience made her sad and afraid.

The tentacles that had originally appeared to float in the air, as if suspended in a gently rolling sea, were now encased within five large mechanical legs resembling those of a robotic crab or spider. Heavy joint assemblies were located at intervals along each leg, giving each a great deal of flexibility and protection. Behind each segment of the mechanical legs, a cluster of tentacles was visible, bundled together, providing the source of motive power for each of the massive legs.

"Chronowarriors!" the voice boomed out, "the humans are in hiding as I have foreseen. Find the Artifex Temporis and bring it to me!"

"Wait!" It was Pax's voice. Pax stepped out from behind the pile of hay at the base of the hill below Möbius. The closest Chronowarrior advanced quickly at Pax, its shining scimitar blade pointed firmly down toward the ground and out at an angle. Within steps from Pax, a red blur shot across his field of vision from his right side. The blur ended in a loud crack as it contacted the side of the Chronowarrior's head. The scimitar that the giant wielded fell to the ground, producing a muffled peal that hung in the air. He followed the sword to the ground and saw the red fletching of one of Veronica's blunt-tipped hunting arrows. Relieved that she had not wasted one of Eckhardt's special creations, Pax was once again amazed at Veronica's archery skills. He recalled having tried to shoot an empty glass container with one of these very same types of blunt arrows; he missed many times from less than ten meters away. Veronica had just delivered a damaging shot from over forty meters at a very difficult angle of declination.

Pax raised his sights up to the Chronowarrior that had stopped in its tracks and towered over him.

A clear blue fluid streamed from an opening at the base of the soldier's neck; the glint of metal showed through this same gash. As a very antiseptic smell filled the air, Pax saw the white glow of the giant's eyes fade to gray.

It was at that moment that Pax realized that these giants were robots, mechanical automatons, and not gigantic humanoid beings.

"Halt!" thundered Möbius. The word was clearly in English, but it seemed to be accompanied by a series of strange sounds.

"Where are the others?" Möbius asked. The main cage of his torso rotated side to side on the base as a human body would if it were looking to each side. The movement seemed silly considering the eyes on the pyramid continued to spin, scanning everything in sight. Pax wondered if this were some programming artifact or if the movement actually had no relation to sight but served some other unknown purpose.

"That doesn't matter," Pax spoke calmly and firmly to a degree that surprised even himself. "What does matter is that the Artifex Temporis is close by."

Pax noticed that the eye began to spin even faster. A visible green glow emanated within the clear ovoid; he wondered if the pyramid floated within some chemiluminescent gas or fluid.

"Give it to me!" thundered Möbius.

"Send your soldiers away," Pax replied.

"You're in no position to make demands," Möbius replied.

"I am if you ever want to see the Artifex again," Pax responded.

"I have the Artifex floating on a piece of hickory in a vat of acid right now. The pH is adjusted such that if I don't retrieve it within about an hour, the wood will dissolve and the Artifex will sink into the vat and rapidly begin to dissolve as well."

Pax had not really thought through the science of the scenario he had just described and had blurted this out to distract Möbius. The pyramid spun even faster. Veins of pulsating orange fluid swirled within the phosphorescent green.

"How foolish," Möbius responded. Pax again detected the sense of desperation in that voice. While this seemed like it was working in his favor at the moment, he was not unaware that the situation could rapidly change. Desperation could swiftly lead to erratic and unpredictable behavior.

"Very well, Pax," Möbius conceded, "I'll play along with your game. Remember, no matter what your plan, I know how this ends. I have seen the future."

Hearing his name spoken by Möbius sent a chill down his spine.

Möbius began to emit a series of strange sounds that oscillated between low clicks and high pings, followed by pulses of light individually directed at each of the Chronowarriors. One by one, each vanished in a flicker of violet radiance until Pax stood alone with Möbius.

In an amazingly rapid series of movements, Möbius descended the hill and stood towering over Pax, leaning unnervingly close. Pax leaned away from the bizarre being, but could not step back too far because one of the metallic crab legs was firmly planted into the ground behind his own.

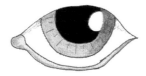

Veronica had panicked when she rounded the windmill and caught her first glimpse of Möbius towering over the cluster of giants on those metallic, crustacean legs.

She had responded quickly when seeing one of these giants move toward Pax with a sword, stopping him in his tracks with a red-fletched *frou-frou* and then quickly retreating out of sight on the windmill's platform.

Isaiah-Jung also ducked out of sight and quietly called out to her from above as if reading her mind, "Veronica, the tentacles are still there. They just appear to be sectioned into clusters and protected by the armor plating forming those legs.

"The tentacles are exposed on the inside. Can you see the unprotected areas?"

Veronica squinted and focused on the two legs farthest from her. Indeed, she could see the mottled flesh of the tentacles. Möbius was sporadically raising and lowering each leg and making various gestures. She saw the terrifying group of soldiers surrounding Möbius and guessed that his leg motions were directed at the soldiers forming the circle.

"This makes it much harder, Isaiah-Jung," Veronica whispered loudly. "I have to shoot through the front legs and strike that very thin opening in the metal exoskeleton."

"You can do it, Veronica." Isaiah-Jung's voice was calm, and the confidence did not sound forced. "Just wait for Pax's signal."

"Thanks. It would be a little easier if that *thing* would stop moving," she replied.

"Go ahead and position yourself for the shot," Isaiah-Jung said. "We need to be ready; we can't miss our opportunity."

As Veronica positioned herself, the soldiers began to disappear in puffs of purple light. Pax and Möbius were soon alone. Before she could even focus on the mechanical legs, they went into a flurry of activity, and Möbius seemed to pounce almost directly onto Pax. This was becoming far more dangerous than she had expected.

"Get ready to take your shot, Veronica, as soon as Pax gives the signal."

Veronica studied the scene. She could not tell if Möbius was holding Pax tightly, preventing him from holding up the fake Artifex, which was her signal to shoot. She was nervous and scared but soon drifted into her focus state where the outside world drifted away and the only thing that remained in her vision was a tunnel between her and her target.

Möbius raised his back leg, which was closest to her, and she almost loosed the arrow, but the leg lowered again, blocking a shot. Seconds later, the leg started to rise again, and Veronica saw Pax's arm raise to the sky.

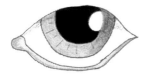

"Where is it?" Möbius shouted.

"Actually, I have it right here," Pax replied, mustering up enough confidence to keep his voice from quivering. "You really didn't think I would jeopardize the Artifex, did you?"

He reached beneath one of the plates of his armor and removed the fake Artifex. As Möbius straightened, Pax thrust the golden piece into the air between them.

Möbius was caught off guard and took a few steps back. The ever-spinning eye focused intently on the gilded object.

"At last! The Artifex is mine once again!" Möbius exclaimed.

Pax thought back to when Möbius said the Artifex had been stolen from him. He had decided this was the ranting of a delusional being, a being with a god complex. Still, the thought of when Möbius could have held possession of the real Artifex Temporis lingered in the back of his mind. Granted, his mother had hidden the Artifex Temporis from him, but she had explained that she had somehow known that it was part of his destiny. Surely if his mother had known anything of Möbius, she would not have kept this information from him. Well, Pax decided, if she had hidden anything from him, it was because she had believed it was in his best interest.

The array of mechanical legs splayed outward and lowered, thrusting the spinning eye of Möbius forward and very close to Pax. Möbius grabbed the counterfeit Artifex, pushing Pax aside in the process. He held the golden prize up in front of his the revolving pyramid, the eye clearly focusing on the shining object.

Pax observed that the speed at which the pyramid spun slowed drastically. As Möbius palmed the piece, the poorly constructed hinge gave way, and the front of the fake Artifex fell to the ground. With the magnet fully exposed, it flew out of Möbius's hand and slammed against the front of his mechanical torso. The strong magnetic field held it firmly against the metal frame.

Möbius's armored legs jerked erratically. The spinning pyramid came to a complete stop with the eyes wide open.

Like the pyramid, the rest of Möbius fell immobile. Pax thought of the anguish that Veronica was facing. He had been studying the armor while Möbius had been standing so close and thought he had spotted a weakness that could help her out. Had he known that the fake Artifex would immobilize Möbius so quickly and completely, he would have carried a syringe of the viral cocktail and injected it directly into the tentacles himself. He wished he had confidence that Möbius was permanently out of commission.

Stepping quickly into the midst of the motionless being, he noticed a series of large yellow levers and deduced that these served as bindings to secure tentacles within the armor. Banking on this observation, he attacked the closest lever. The lever did not even budge initially, and Pax doubted both his theory and his ability to free these levers. Stars spread across his vision from his exerting so much effort, but Pax finally felt the lever give way and pop open. Catching his breath and squeezing his eyes tightly shut for a moment, he moved onto the next binding and found it much easier. Pax was able to free the remainder of the bindings on each armored leg, each easier to open than the prior. He moved from the top to the bottom of all five legs, and the armor fell away from each of the first four legs by the time the last lever opened. Several tentacles remained entwined within the hinges and supports of one of the rear legs.

Thickly and heavily, the unrestricted tentacles spread open, pushing Pax back against the opposing legs, but they still showed no sign of activity. Möbius's ovoid body slowly listed forward as the last cluster of tentacles were freed, but still remained upright. Pax studied the legs closely but could not be certain as to whether they were organic or synthetic in nature. How could any organic material possibly survive the forces needed to accomplish time travel? Or was Möbius actually able to actually achieve time travel? Hesitant to actually touch the flesh that sprawled out around him, he peered closely at the surface of the skin, trying to determine its nature. Curiosity finally overcame him, and he ran his fingers over an area of the mottled gray and red membrane, gently at first, and then much firmer. The skin was dry and coarser than Pax had expected based on its moist and slimy appearance. The fiber of the tentacle was very dense, as well.

Pax placed both hands beneath a tentacle, planning to lift it up, but jerked back quickly. Large suction cups covered the underside of the tentacle, each ringed with sharp, fibrous bristle. He once again moved to lift a single tentacle from among the large coil of those that had splayed out of the open armor. Trying to isolate a single arm caused a cluster of several to slide over, their weight forcing Pax backward.

As Pax was pushed back, he looked up at the base that supported the clear ovoid above. For the most part, all he could see was a mass of fibrous tissue where the legs entered the base of the metal cage that framed Möbius. Standing in the shadow of the umbrella of flesh and alloy, a series of strange markings caught his eye, and he leaned in to take a closer look. The markings were writing, in English.

"Morphogenetic-Ovoidal Extraterrestrial Bathyscaphic Instrument: Unified States" was clearly inscribed on the inner lip of the metal ring that encircled the base. Beneath it was a plate that said "serial number" with a string of information following. As he paused to consider the meaning of this information and strained to look for more information, Möbius began to stir, ever so slightly. He heard machinery whirring to life and felt Möbius begin to move. Pax moved quickly to get out so Veronica could take her shot at the exposed tentacles. He wished she had taken a shot while the creature had been stationary but knew that she would not risk it while he was positioned within the mass of metal legs and flaccid arms.

As Pax stepped out from the living cage that surrounded him, Möbius began to move more visibly. The hideous pyramid containing the four eyes began to spin again and Möbius turned slowly to follow Pax. The being's movements were still slow and uncoordinated, but Pax could tell that the paralytic effects were temporary and that Möbius would be fully functional very shortly.

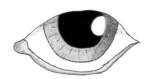

Veronica had seen the glint of shining gold as Pax had held the Artifex up toward Möbius. This triggered Veronica to set the string of her bow free, but as she had verified her aim, she saw Pax step beneath Möbius. She quickly checked herself and slowly released the tension from the bowstring, leaving the arrow to rest on the shelf of the bow. She watched for Möbius to react to Pax's movement. The creature stood completely unmoving.

After the fake Artifex had paralyzed Möbius, Isaiah-Jung had scrambled down the stairs and was now sprinting toward Pax. Veronica was certain that he had said something on his way out, but she had been so focused on her aim and concerned for Pax that she could not recall what it was now. She watched as Isaiah-Jung quickly covered the distance between the windmill and where Möbius stood immobilized, with Pax obscured from view beneath.

It seemed like an eternity that Pax moved beneath that monster, but he eventually emerged. Möbius had begun to stir and had followed Pax's movement as he emerged. Her line of sight to the tentacles was once again blocked by the armor that stood haphazardly surrounding Möbius.

As she watched the scene below, instead of fleeing, Pax began to move clockwise around Möbius. Veronica saw that he was luring Möbius in a circle and knew that Pax was trying to draw Möbius away from the wall of metallic legs that were clearly a barrier between this creature and the windmill, positioning the target for her shot. She quickly aimed and loosed the arrow as the tentacles moved into clear view.

Time flowed at a glacial pace after the bowstring slipped from her index and middle finger. Veronica found herself attempting to psychically will the course of the arrow. She could feel the vibration of the bowstring against her right cheek and a slight sting spreading across her face, but she stood unblinking, watching the arrow sail. In what seemed like minutes, Möbius's rear leg, onto which the armor erratically dangled, began an upward arc. The spinning eyes did not register the approaching threat.

For a brief second, Veronica wondered if Möbius was actually aware of the oncoming arrow and was simply confident that it was not a threat, or if he had just not detected it. She pushed that thought out of her mind and decided to ready another arrow.

Never dropping her eyes from Möbius and Pax, she knocked the arrow. As she reached forward to remove the cork, she saw the arrow pass just beneath the last segment of the sole semi-armored legs and strike the exposed flesh of the closest unprotected tentacle waving beyond. Only seconds had elapsed.

The arrow remained!

The eyes seemed to slow and hesitate. She wondered if Möbius was trying to determine the origin of the arrow.

She saw Pax fall to the ground and roll.

In the next instant, the haystack beside Möbius exploded. Veronica knew that Eckhardt had launched his viral mortar. Sparks sprayed from the opposite side of Möbius that was out of her view, and she saw a spray of yellow fluid erupt from the mortar. Rivulets of the fluid rolled off of the clear egg-shaped body of Möbius.

A siren sound filled the air. Sören and Sasha had activated the beacon.

Veronica watched, elated by the successfully execution of their plan, waiting for Möbius to fall immobile once again from their three-way assault. Möbius's tentacles flailed about in an agitated state, and his torso spun sharply toward the windmill, directly facing Isaiah-Jung as he crested the small hill only meters away from Möbius, still running full speed.

As Isaiah-Jung tried to stop, a tentacle shot out and quickly ensnared him. Isaiah-Jung's feet came off of the ground and he was whipped violently through the air as if he was a piece of cloth.

Veronica winced as a blinding violet flash of light erupted.

Möbius once again vanished.

Isaiah-Jung was gone.

CHAPTER FOURTEEN
(A new, old friend)

Dhaal grabbed Agathi's hand and started running. He was moving directly away from the Chronomicon, and Agathi was gripped with panic as she saw nothing but the open and desolate plains spreading out into darkness before them. Abruptly, Dhaal changed direction and veered directly back toward the Chronomicon, where Möbius and legions of the giant robot soldiers were moving in their direction.

Agathi wondered if Dhaal had lost his mind.

"Where are you going, Dhaal?" Agathi called out.

"Just follow," Dhaal gasped. "I think we have only one hope."

Dhaal was moving fast, but Agathi did not think he could keep up this pace for long.

The two were moving directly toward one of the larger sets of statues on the periphery of the enormous pit. Off to the sides in the distance, Agathi could see rows of glowing white eyes as the soldiers began making their ascent up the ramps to the side of the Chronomicon.

She could now see what Dhaal had done by taking such a seemingly erratic course. He had moved directly away from Möbius and down the tor so they would immediately be out of sight, their followers hopefully thinking they were choosing to flee across the plain. But then he had doubled back using the largest set of statues to block them from view. That would work until the soldiers below crested the top of the depression, which both Agathi and Dhaal could see they were rapidly approaching.

The statues quickly rose up in front of them as they approached the brink. Dhaal carefully peered around the statue and was met with the eerie scene created by the myriad illuminated eyes glowing in the pit. The blackness outside of the Chronomicon seemed to grow heavier. Dhaal could barely distinguish Agathi when he moved back into the darkness.

"We'll use these statues to move down into the pit," Dhaal said confidently.

"What?" Agathi called out, much louder than she had intended. She was certain that the older man was delirious now. "That's where the robots are," she gasped.

"That's where they *were* Agathi. It's our only chance," Dhaal responded, "We cannot outrun these machines across the plain. We need to hide long enough for this to recharge so we can go back." Dhaal held up the cuirass. Agathi could barely see a faint glow on the gauge.

"It seems to be taking a long time to recharge," she said.

"Maybe all of our friends are taking all the available energy."

Dhaal had stepped into the gap separating the two enormous statues. Positioning his feet between the two and using his walking staff to balance, he looked up and tried to make out the top of the statues above him, but they rose too high into the darkness. He knew that they could not be seen if they stayed in this space and worked their way down.

Dhaal gestured for Agathi to join him on what appeared to be the carved sash of the giant knight depicted in stone. The pair cautiously made their way down. Dhaal slipped and slid for quite a distance as the sash took a downward turn, but was eventually saved by what he guessed was a gigantic carved spur. As he lay on his back, racked with pain, he guessed that he was at the base of an enormous boot that towered overhead.

Agathi caught up with him, moving far more gracefully. Dhaal was slowly standing, using the broken section of his walking stick to which he still clung. She helped him up the rest of the way, and the two stood together on the spur, just a few meters above the thick mist that carpeted the ground below. A slight glow emanated from the mist. Veins of white light coursed up the angled ramps leading out of the Chronomicon. Agathi was still baffled by the sheer number of the figures. The forward progress of these soldiers was beginning to get unnervingly close, and although they were far below the path of the soldiers, she felt they needed to get farther out of sight.

Dhaal began to ease his way down into the mist, hanging momentarily from the spur. He then completely let go. He dropped into the cottony shroud below, and Agathi heard a muted splash.

It was silent for a few moments, and she felt that sense of panic returning. What if something happened to Dhaal?

"Hurry. Come in," she heard Dhaal whisper, and she reluctantly followed him in, disappearing into the mist.

Agathi dropped through the white blanket and landed on a hard but flexible surface. She realized that she was now sitting on one of the clear panels that she had seen from above. Just below, she could see Dhaal, standing waist-deep in water.

Agathi slid off the edge of the clear panel and dropped into the water below.

Dhaal and Agathi stood in very warm water, bordering on uncomfortable. The bed of the lake or pond in which they stood was smooth and hard. At first, Dhaal thought he had had the good fortune to land on a flat, level rock, but after only a few steps, he realized that this was not a natural lake.

"This is man-made," Dhaal said. "Well, at least it isn't natural," he corrected himself. He wasn't exactly certain who had made this reservoir. He moved his hands through the water and sensed that it was heavily aerated.

Sweat already dripped from both Dhaal and Agathi's faces, and the humidity was nearly stifling. The heavy mist surrounding them seemed like a living thing, ebbing and moving, on occasion completely blocking their sight of the water in which they stood.

Dhaal caught a glimpse across the surface of the steam to the opposite side of the Chronomicon, and followed the trails of white eyes that marched up and out of this canyon. Dhaal and Agathi were far away from one of these ramparts and it seemed safe enough to move forward if they stayed low within the mist. Dhaal's hair was white like the mist, so he felt comfortable, and Agathi was shorter than he, and the white gossamer humidity seemed to blanket her golden hair well enough. The white light in the center, from below where Möbius had hovered when they first looked into the Chronomicon, still glowed in his absence. The two glanced at each other and nodded before moving in that direction.

Agathi was struck by the immensity of this space. Spanning hundreds of meters across, this was the largest "man made" structure Agathi had ever seen.

Fanning herself did not help, and the heat was starting to make her dizzy. Agathi was beginning to see stars, when Dhaal came to an abrupt stop. She heard water lapping in front of them.

She heard more movement in the water and heard Dhaal whisper, "A wall. Feels like a metal grate on the other side."

She saw Dhaal rise up out of the water and roll over onto the grating. He reached back and lifted Agathi easily out of the water. The grating was at the same level as the water, and Agathi felt a wave of coolness from below. It was still muggy, but the flow of air over her at least hinted at a sense of refreshment.

"I thought I was being boiled alive," she gasped quietly.

"Yes, it was warm, but it felt good on the joints of an old man."

Dark skies still loomed above, but the closer they moved toward the center, the brighter their surroundings became. A light was emanating from below the metal grate, but all the pair could see below was more steam.

Dhaal used the remainder of his hiking staff to feel in front of him as he walked forward, checking for more walls, obstacles, or openings.

The grid that supported them was metal, like steel, but had a rough surface that gave them sure footing, even dripping with water and sweat. It was ribbed with gaps large enough for Agathi to fit her hand through, but with no danger of her foot slipping in between as long as she moved at a ninety-degree angle across the ribs.

Presently, Dhaal and Agathi became aware of a low hum. How long had the sound been present? Both of them could actually feel the vibration in the metal grating resonating in harmony with the sound. The vibration fluctuated in between two distinct patterns, indicating that it was produced by something cycling at a steady rate. The two interlopers moved silently across.

Agathi had been staring directly down, watching her feet as she followed with her left hand on Dhaal's shoulder. She had noticed a pattern in the grating; as they moved forward, the joints between the large panels of metal grating were appearing more frequently and at more severe angles. In her mind, she assembled a mental picture of this platform they traversed: she envisioned the large circular canyon with a barrier of water between the edge and the beginning of this platform. Based on the angles of the grating and the patterns formed by the joints, she saw this structure as an octagon. The center of her mental image was as diffuse and formless as the luminous white steam that enshrouded them.

Agathi began to catch a glimpse of the substructure beneath them and realized that the steam was thinning. Massive beams and pillars supported this deck and faded into the deeper recesses below. She produced a mental diagram of where they stood; she saw the surface of the plain across which they had fled earlier and pictured that stepping down to the ledge that held a mote of steaming water. The section ended at the wall where the grate began, which dropped downward to some undefined depth.

Agathi wondered what surprises waited ahead.

Her question was soon answered as she saw a railing appear before them. The mist was nearly gone here, and she saw that the rail formed a circle that had a diameter of only about thirty meters. Short staircases formed of the same material as the grating were positioned at about five meter intervals all the way around, dropping down onto another deck about ten meters below. They moved to the opening of one of these stairways, and Dhaal began to descend. Agathi followed.

They were struck by the scale of the stairs—not abnormally steep, but the distance between each step was twice that she would normally expect. This made descending an awkward process, and it was more easily done when turned backward, like climbing down a ladder.

"These stairs were designed for those giant soldiers, I gather," said Dhaal as he reached the bottom and stood stretching out his aching back. Agathi nodded in agreement, still feeling slightly light-headed.

Large yellow cylinders with horizontally segmented doors of bare shining metal were located around this lower deck, recessed beneath the decking above.

Agathi observed that these were positioned evenly between the staircases that connected the two levels.

Intensely bright lights hung beneath this deck and illuminated a concrete silo that dropped another hundred meters; it was difficult for Agathi to judge such depth while standing directly above.

Spokes of concrete were visible toward the lower end of this silo, radiating to the center where they joined in a hub.

Agathi moved over to one of the tall yellow cylinders. To the right side of the door, at about her eye level, was a large, flat panel, the only feature on the cylinder with the exception of the door. She placed her hand on the panel and pushed.

The door began to rise.

Agathi jumped at first, startled by the movement. She realized that she had expected the door to open but was still surprised when it actually did.

She stepped back and stood by Dhaal, waiting to see what was inside.

The chamber was large and octagonal in shape, probably large enough for twenty or so people. *Well, twenty people of my size,* Agathi thought. The floor was a solid sheet of metal, not the grating like everywhere else, and two conveyor belts were perpendicular to the door. Agathi could only guess that these were to move something heavy from the back of the elevator out of the door.

She watched as Dhaal stepped inside. Agathi quickly moved in as well, not wanting to be left alone if the door suddenly slammed shut. The ceiling was high as she expected, assuming this too was scaled for the massive soldiers. Several bars ran overhead from the back wall to the front, perpendicular to the door. She could not hazard a guess as to their function.

An array of buttons lined an interior panel by the door; their purpose seemed obvious.

"It seems empty," Dhaal said. "I guess there is no need for any security here."

"I can't imagine anyone wanting to get in," Agathi replied. It was cooler in here, and she was finally starting to feel herself again.

"We might as well look around," Dhaal said, dropping the shoulder of his robe to reveal the cuirass underneath, the light from gauge still barely visible. "It doesn't look like we're leaving soon."

"And with all of those monsters headed out," Agathi jerked her thumb over her shoulder, "I'll take my chances here. But we shouldn't overstay our welcome. Eventually they'll give up looking for us and return."

Dhaal depressed the first button and the elevator began to descend. Agathi and Dhaal stood watching bare concrete rising up before them.

Expecting the door to have closed, Dhaal and Agathi just looked at each other and shrugged.

Moving quickly, the car arrived at the next level and came to a gradual stop. Agathi pictured this to be the point at which the concrete spoke radiated out from the silo wall.

Agathi gasped and grabbed Dhaal. Appearing before them as the car descended were pairs of the same armored boots worn by the giant soldiers. Pair after pair came into view as the car continued to slow. She watched as the legs followed, expecting a garrison to be waiting to capture them, or worse.

She looked around for anything to use as a weapon, but there was nothing inside the sterile elevator. As she turned back toward the doorway, preparing to fight hand-to-hand, she stopped.

Rows of the giant soldiers were standing at attention, forming a corridor that moved out from the elevator, but the only thing they were waiting for was to be assembled or repaired. The boots and legs that had terrified her were about the extent of many of these fierce warriors, and in some cases were the only parts present.

Light from the elevator reflected off of the mechanical internal workings of the robots. Each stood supported by a cable secured to a hook at the waist of each. Dhaal moved within the various configurations of the robotics, looking intently at the arrangement of the gears, touching the fabric, occasionally moving one of the mechanical arms. He did not see a cuirass anywhere in sight.

"This must be where Möbius manufacturers the robot soldiers," Agathi said.

A row of the fake heads and torsos hung limply on racks behind the robots. Without the glowing white eyes, they looked even more lifeless, if that were possible, each face and hairpiece identical to the next. Agathi wondered why Möbius went to all of the trouble to make these robots look humanoid. If he planned to take over their world after securing the Artifex Temporis, why was he concerned with their appearance at all? And why did he need so many? Granted, Dhaal had gained an advantage on one by using the Artifex Temporis, but legions of these warriors would be unstoppable. Her society was not a warlike people, nor did Agathi believe many military peoples remained after the Ecology Wars.

"Möbius wants to be worshipped in addition to having military strength," Dhaal interrupted Agathi's thoughts. He was staring directly at her, seemingly reading her mind. "Your expression and intensity speaks volumes," Dhaal said in response to her look.

"He wants to be worshipped by many, apparently," Agathi said. "But if that's what they're programmed to do and have no choice, they do not really worship him."

"He has delusions of grandeur and believes himself a god," Dhaal stated, "I do not believe he is concerned with freewill."

"The strange thing about these," Dhaal made a sweeping gesture toward the lifeless carcasses of the robot soldiers, "is the absence of a power source." Dhaal's brow was furrowed, and he scratched at one side of the flowing mustache that rested on his shoulder.

A noise made them both jump.

"They've returned," Agathi whispered.

"No. I believe the sound came from below," Dhaal replied.

They moved quickly back to the elevator and pressed the next button in the series. The car began its descent.

No soldiers assembled or in disrepair awaited them below. The light was much dimmer here, but a distinct smell wafted in to the elevator to meet them. The smell was that of humans.

Faint voices were immediately silenced as the elevator came to rest. The pair stepped cautiously out of the doorway of the elevator, peering into the dim light and waiting for their eyes to adjust.

Agathi pressed her back against the chilly wall and moved away from the elevator, feeling cautiously ahead of her. Soon she encountered a bank of switches. She tentatively flipped one, bracing herself for some blaring siren or security measure, but was met only with a cluster of lights flickering to life above her. She continued to flip switches and watched lights erratically wake up down the length of the hall.

It looked like a prison. Barred doors lined both sides as far down as they could see. All of the lights above still did not make the corridor seem bright. A dull, milky green color covered the walls, barred doors, and ceiling. The floors were a faded black color; warped and uneven areas could be seen sporadically up and down the length of its surface.

Dhaal and Agathi began inching down the hallway.

Forms cowered in the light that now blazed from above the cells: human forms. The thick bars on each door ran horizontally and were spaced far enough apart for an average-sized man to easily fit an arm through the gap.

Registering that these two passing by their cells were fellow humans and not the towering cloned robots, the people within began to rise up to their feet and rush the doors that held them contained within.

"Help us!" they cried. "Let us out!"

"Who are you?"

"Where are you from?"

The question and calls for help poured from the cells and flooded the hallway like the water from a broken dam.

Agathi was disoriented by the sound and covered her ears. Through her muffled ears, she could discern many different languages calling out, many of which she did not recognize.

The litany continued on. People called out family names and inquired about ones obviously left behind, wherever behind was.

Dhaal raised his arms. He spoke out, "Be silent and silence those beside you. You will only call back your captors with your cries!" He repeated this in several languages, occasionally with an impressive fluency, but mostly with a rudimentary simplicity. Agathi guessed that he utilized every language he knew.

Gradually, the din subsided. Dhaal moved farther down the hallway to the middle of the corridor. "Who here speaks *this* language? Is there one here in charge?" he called out firmly, without shouting. He had never seen a collective group where one individual didn't gravitate, either voluntarily or reluctantly, to assume the role of the leader.

Several voices rang out at the same time, and hands jutted from behind the bars waving frantically. It took a while, but Dhaal sorted out the name Hague and determined that the waving hands were directing him farther down toward the end of the passage.

Dhaal and Agathi moved in that direction. As they walked, Agathi studied the structure of the cells. Each barred door had a single hinge at the top, which cantilevered to a motor mounted on the ceiling. No bolts or locks were present, and she concluded the motor itself served as the mechanism to keep the door secured. She also gathered that it would not normally have been a good idea to slip out of these doors when the robotic soldiers stood watch. She could imagine feeling safer on the other side of these bars when those monsters were policing the grounds.

"Hague?" Dhaal asked as he reached the end cell.

"I used to be," a rough voice replied. "And who are you?"

"Friends, I believe," said Dhaal. "My name is Dhaal. And this is Agathi." He bowed slightly. Agathi had walked up beside Dhaal and did a slight curtsy.

Like a bolt of lightning, Hague's arm reached out and grabbed Agathi by the neck. Dhaal reacted quickly and drove Hague's arm down hard against the bars with his elbow.

Hague yelped and fell back grimacing, rubbing his elbow.

"Sorry, old fella. I just wanted to check for body heat. I've been surrounded by these cold-blooded clones for too many years. I've grown not to trust anyone, and wanted to make sure you two weren't just newer models."

Agathi rubbed her neck and held up her hand to show that she was fine.

"Understandable," she squeaked out. "Can we agree to work together without any further tests, though?"

"Works for me," Hague replied.

"How do we set you free?"

The man had obviously contemplated that very question for some time.

"I know these two cells open first when we go out to work," Hague described, pointing to the cell across and then to his. "And then the guards come out at this end." He jerked his thumb to the door directly to Dhaal's left, only a few meters away. "I'd guess you'll find the controls through there."

"Where did all the guards go?" Hague asked.

"Looking for us," Agathi smiled.

"I should have guessed," Hague replied. "You both have some moxie marching in here like this."

"Sometimes the best hiding place is in plain sight," the elder man commented and winked.

Dhaal turned and stood before the two doors. He was looking around for something to leverage them open, when Agathi just reached out and pushed. The doors opened without resistance.

"Always taking the easy way out," Dhaal said facetiously, somewhat embarrassed that he had not even tried that approach.

"Never know if you don't try," Agathi retorted.

"Touché," Dhaal said as he moved through into a small room that had an identical set of double doors on the opposite side. An array of levers stood on the far wall, each with a red indicator above it.

"Doesn't get much easier than this," Dhaal said. Agathi grimaced, thinking back to these same words used by one of the bandits years ago when she had posed as a helpless young bride leaving Orneth. That seemed like a lifetime ago.

Dhaal walked over to the panel. "Why don't you watch down the hallway and tell me if the doors begin to open."

He picked a lever and pulled. A whirr began down the hallway, followed by a shout of relief and joy. Agathi could see the barred door rising up to the ceiling at the far end.

"Keep going," she called back to Dhaal over her shoulder and then turned to help him with the levers.

Soon the hallway was crowded with the freed prisoners and filled with excited chatter.

"I suggest you send your men out while the robots are gone," Dhaal said to Hague.

"I don't think they need me to tell them to leave this place," Hague replied. "What about you?"

"We're looking for something to help us against Möbius and the soldiers in our world," Dhaal said.

"I can help you there," Hague replied. "And maybe you can help us all get back to your world… *our* world." Hague said with a distant look in his eyes.

"You need to disable the source of their energy," Hague said, "That's what powers them all—the robots at least. I don't know about the four-eyed squid," Hague said, his lips pursed in disgust. "I think he might have his own power supply."

"I noticed that the robots don't have an internal power supply." Dhaal slapped Hague's shoulder. "They are powered by a single, remote source. Somewhere here, I gather."

"A monk and an engineer," Hague scoffed. "The supply is farther down, a few levels below."

"You go while you can. You've spent enough time in this place." Dhaal patted him on the shoulder. "We'll take it from here."

"Sixteen years, one month, and seven days," Hague said, the anger sharpening the accent of each number. "That's how long I've been held here.

"You all just saved my life," Hague continued. "And besides, I'm not really even sure where we are or how to get back, so you're not going anywhere without me. I'm just a worried about being trapped down here if they start pouring back in above us."

"If this can transport all three, I think we're safe," Dhaal exposed the cuirass to Hague. "Assuming it regains a charge."

"Those things are what we need to get back?" Hague looked surprised. "I wish I'd known that all this time; I would have found some way to get my hands on one of those a long time ago."

"These allow us to move back and forth – we think between parallel dimensions. Although it takes some time for them to recharge after each use," Dhaal concluded.

"Well, you're at the main power source, the mother lode," Hague responded. "You should have plenty of power."

"We'll go this way," Hague pointed back through the double doors. "I think the elevators to the surface will be busy for a while."

Dhaal looked back at the line of animated prisoners, anxiously fidgeting and shuffling in the corridor, waiting for their ride to freedom.

"We'll have to find a way to come back for them," Dhaal said, turning away.

Agathi followed Dhaal and Hague, something weighing heavily on her mind. Every time she thought she had put her finger on it, it slipped away. All of a sudden, she stopped and called to Hague.

"Are you from Orneth?" she asked. "Do you have a son?"

"Yes, I am," he replied. "And I did have a baby son just before I was captured and brought here."

"What was his name?"

"Pax," he replied.

Tears welled up in her eyes. Agathi ran to Hague and threw her arms around him.

"Pax is my best friend! He's leading us all to protect the Artifex Temporis and to fight Möbius!"

Hague looked shocked. Emotions swirling in his soul were clearly manifest in his face and eyes.

"Where is he? Is he here with you?" Hague blurted out.

"He's back in Orneth," Agathi answered. "We were captured by the soldiers as well."

"We should keep moving," Dhaal interrupted.

"You're right. Let's go," Hague said and continued on. He came to a ladder and practically slid down its entire length. "Follow me," he called up.

By the time Dhaal and Agathi made it down, Hague was standing at a bulkhead spinning the large wheel that opened the latch.

"This way. Hurry!" he waved as he stepped though the threshold.

The group stepped out onto another platform.

"This is the reactor," Hague stated.

"What?" Agathi gasped. "Möbius is using a nuclear reactor as his power source?" she cried out, obviously mortified. The idea that a nuclear reactor even existed after the Ecology War was unfathomable, much less that someone was actually starting one up to use as a routine power source.

"All the energy for the Chronomicon comes from the reactor," Hague called out. "And they need a lot of power. Disrupt the power flowing from the reactor, and the robots are dead, useless.

"I believe the power is transmitted from the tower above. I know that each robot has a receiver assembly located in its torso."

"How do you know so much about the robots?" Agathi asked.

"That's why we were brought here," Hague went on, "to help build this place, to build and repair robots. And I've spent far too much time observing these things."

"How do we disrupt the output from a reactor?" Dhaal asked.

"We could damage it with some explosives," Hague responded. "I have an idea where we might find some."

"We just need to make sure that we can get far away from here before we breach a reactor," Agathi observed. "We also need to avoid those robots; we saw how strong they are."

"That's another thing," Hague responded. "I think the more of the Chronowarriors that are activated, the weaker each one becomes."

"That makes sense, since they are sharing a power source," Agathi commented.

"Where would those explosives you mentioned be, Hague?" Dhaal asked.

"Farther down," Hague said. "I haven't been below the reactor level but have heard plenty of explosions echoing up from the down there. I have no idea what they're up to."

"Why don't you two wait here, and I'll go look."

"Let's just stick together," Dhaal said calmly. That settled that.

The trio quickly moved into an elevator designated for the lower floors, and Hague pressed the very bottom button on the interior panel. Down they went.

CHAPTER FIFTEEN
(Connections made)

The OCL gathered at Eckhardt's small hut behind his family home. Relatively small, this room did not incorporate any of the metal beams or glass reclaimed from the aftermath of the Ecology War. White stone walls defined the space and dark wooden beams stretched across the top and supported the large slabs of slate that formed the roof.

The group sat reviewing what had happened and generally reconnoitering after their recent encounter with Möbius.

"I can't believe that not one of the three approaches worked," Eckhardt said, shaking his head.

"They might have, Eck," Sören said. "All three were viral strategies and could take some time to have an effect."

"But the viral cocktail in the arrow that Veronica launched also contained a powerful neurotoxin that should have caused instant paralysis; it produced no effect at all."

"It seems the magnet in the fake Artifex that was the only thing really effective," Pax commented.

"That gives me an idea," Eck said and began scouring through some files.

"That's a surprise," someone said facetiously.

Pax continued, "When I stepped underneath Möbius to try and loosen the segments that were protecting the tentacles, I noticed writing around the base of that metal cage area," Pax tried to indicate a comparable area near his own waist.

Very little information existed about encounters with any alien intelligence, and what was available was marginal at best. Several in the group were thinking that a new written language might provide some clues to another life form from somewhere in the universe.

"The writing was in English."

"English? That's odd, don't you think?" Sören asked rhetorically.

"What did it say?" asked Sasha.

"In one area it said 'Deep Space Colonization Project.' That wasn't so odd; that was an ongoing project that I think we've all at least heard about in history class," Pax said. "But it was the next part that was so interesting. I remember this clearly because it was so strange. It said 'Morphogenetic Ovoidal Extraterrestrial Bathyscaphic Instrument.' Each word was capitalized and then there was a dash, and then it said 'Unified States.'"

"Unified States!" Sören gasped. "The Unified States haven't existed since the Ecology Wars concluded, thousands of years ago."

Eck sat pondering a series of sketches that he had pulled from the files he had been rifling through. Talking to himself as much as much as anyone else, he said, "The 'ovoidal' part is pretty obvious from looking at the structure of the clear body, but 'a morphogenetic extraterrestrial bathyscaph?'" Eckhardt rubbed his chin, his mind working in overdrive to make some connections. "I'm going to see if I have any reference data in my database that might help. The digital information available on that period is sketchy. It's still being inputted from the archived books and papers that are available."

Sasha stood and walked over to Eckhardt, carrying a leather-bound book with her. She opened it to a page and pointed out something to him, tapping firmly on the page.

"Möbius!" Veronica yelled out.

At first, everyone jumped, thinking that their nemesis had returned.

"Where?" asked Pax, looking about. Veronica had been sitting on a low table by the window, and he thought that Möbius might be within her view outside.

"No," said Veronica. "Morphogenetic. Ovoidal. Extraterrestrial. Bathyscaphic. Instrument. Unified. States. MOEBIUS!" she explained. "MOEBIUS is an acronym!" Veronica beamed, pleased to have possibly solved the puzzle.

Everyone sighed collectively.

"Nice work, Veronica," said Pax. "It seems so clear now that you said it."

"Most discoveries are like that," said Eckhardt as he moved over to his computer, still mumbling as he walked.

"Still doesn't really make any sense. So we know that the name is an acronym. Does that help?"

"It tells us that us that at least part of Möbius was made by people living in the Unified States, which makes him about three thousand years old, not an artifact from the beginning of time, as Möbius said," Pax responded.

"Or, it tells us that the sentient, thinking part of Möbius used materials from that period to construct a physical body to occupy. Just like we do to build houses and everything else," said Veronica.

"That's an interesting angle," Pax replied.

"So Möbius is a submarine designed to travel out of the galaxy?" Pax asked. "Where does the 'morphogenetic' aspect fit in?"

"Why would anyone want to send a bathyscaph out into the galaxy? That doesn't seem to make any sense," Sören added.

"Unless they were visiting an ocean planet," Eck chimed in. "Or transporting something to another planet, which looks like what they were trying to do."

Holding up the volume Sasha had just handed to him, Eck said, "Sasha has found something extremely interesting from her library."

Eckhardt set the volume down by his monitor and started tapping away at the keyboard. With each keystroke, the glowing green text on his display grew brighter.

"There's not much here but a reference to a project later into the twenty-third century. When the conditions of our oceans were deteriorating and they were becoming increasingly contaminated, a group was testing out a transport for certain sea animals that were threatened. Initially it was used for certain cephalopods that seemed to survive cryogenic storage better than mammals.

Eventually, larger scale container ships were planned for moving dolphins and whales. I can't tell if that ever materialized.

"The interesting part is that these small ships were based on unmanned bathyscaphs that had been developed for deep sea monitoring of areas that were unsafe for humans."

"Monitoring?" Sasha asked as she stood peering over Eck's shoulder.

"Spying would be my guess. Reconnaissance for the Unified States to keep an eye what the Developing States were doing under the sea.

"Anyway," Eckhardt said, directing the group back to his original point. He placed his finger back on the screen, reading the content there. "These ships were utilizing a relatively untested form of artificial intelligence based on a hybrid of computer and organic processors forming a Somatic Kernel—the latest in organic-robotic intelligence at the time. Possibly the most advanced technology ever."

"Organic processors? Does that mean brains?" Veronica asked.

"That would be my guess," Eck replied.

"Human brains?" she asked pointedly with a grimace on her face. Her eyebrows were raised high over her large eyes, and she looked disgusted.

"Can't tell from this information, but I would hazard a guess that they were. A lot of work had been done in the medical field to integrate computer processors into human brains."

He placed Sasha's book under a scanner and enlarged the picture to a size large enough for everyone to easily see. A very simplistic diagram of a transport rocket appeared on the screen.

"These rockets had apparently been originally designed to launch multiple satellites. Look how this picture shows one loaded with a series of these egg-shaped containers," Eck commented.

"Do they all have spinning eyes and tentacles? Or is our Möbius an upgraded model?" Sören asked.

"No. I think we just got lucky," Eck said sarcastically. "Sasha's image here is of one of the ships holding several squid, being loaded onto a rocket for launch." Pax tried to zoom in and enlarge the image. "Some of these ships are much larger than Möbius."

The basic structure of the ship looked practically identical, like Möbius reclining in a wheeled cart being pulled up via a series of cables. Except where the tentacles originated on Möbius, there was an extended cylinder with two propellers and an array of rudders for guiding the vessel while in the water. Assorted stainless steel mandibles and grasping devices protruded from where the humanoid hands were on Möbius. Most noticeably absent was the pyramid with the four eyes. Clearly visible at the top of the dome was a series of communication devices: the curled cord of a hand-held microphone, as well as various groupings of levers to control certain outside tools and light assemblies. Two black plastic seats were positioned back to back farther down in the glass egg. Not a spot for anyone who suffered from claustrophobia.

No spinning eyes.

"This project was for far more than just transporting sea animals; it looks like the real motivation was finding a location to colonize and expand.

"I'm going to toss out a theory that one of these ships evolved into Möbius," Eck said.

"Maybe that one in the picture," Sasha pointed. "It looks like there is a giant squid inside. Maybe that's where the tentacles are from.

"That's quite an evolution."

"I would say that it's more modification and adaptation than evolution. The sentient component of the ship could have been responding to whatever conditions it encountered on the planet where it landed, or to something in flight. If it was intended to go extraterrestrial, it could have been travelling for a long time."

"Was it designed to return? How did it even get back?"

"Möbius seems to have developed some innovative methods of travel," Veronica commented. "We don't know if he can travel in time, but he could have picked up some advanced technology from wherever he visited."

"Obviously. The pyramid with the eyes? I can't even hazard a guess on that part." Veronica threw her hands up in the air in a helpless gesture.

"Maybe the transport encountered a life-form once it arrived at its destination that took control of the ship and made some modifications?"

"Could be, I guess. Maybe some disembodied life-form looking for a home. Like a hermit crab," Eck commented.

Pax sat down on the table by Veronica and drifted off from the current conversations, wondering if he would ever see the Artifex Temporis again, wondering what secrets it held that this enigmatic monster sought it so intently. What disturbed Pax the most was why Dhaal had taken it from him at all, with no explanation?

"Why do you think Dhaal would have taken the Artifex Temporis from me, Veronica?" Pax leaned over and asked softly, not wanting to interrupt the brainstorming of the others. An expression of anguish spread over his face.

"I've been wondering about that, as well," Veronica started. "I think he must have needed it for something. You said he was in quite a hurry, like it was something urgent."

Pax nodded. Veronica always saw the best in everyone and never spoke disparagingly about a person. She always tried to find some redeeming quality in every individual. In this case, Pax was hopeful that she was right. Although he had only known Dhaal for a very short time, he felt that a deep bond had been established due to their circumstances.

"I'm really worried about Agathi and Isaiah-Jung," Veronica said.

"We all are," Pax said, "I had hoped that Agathi was far enough away not to be affected, but seeing Dhaal without her made me think otherwise."

"If he took the Artifex to help her, I hope it works. As for Isaiah-Jung, I just hope Möbius didn't hurt him," Veronica concluded.

"What about the Chronowarriors?" Sasha was asking as Pax focused once again on the remainder of the group.

"I'll bet that they are creations of Möbius," Sören said. "My guess is that Möbius has a factory that produces the Chronowarriors. He seems to have an infinite supply."

"Maybe where he comes from has an infinite amount of resources?" Sasha commented.

"Does someone want to continue looking through this stuff?" Eck said. "I want to take a look at something else that might be helpful." Eck scooped up the sheaf of drawings and papers and walked out of the room.

Sasha took over Eckhardt's seat and began scrolling through the various files related to the hybrid organic processors. A large image of a scientist from the late twenty-third century filled the screen. The image looked very professorial: a high receding hairline, with waves of gray coursing through the hair that remained. Deep, dark eyes stared out, their intensity memorialized in this digital image from thousands of years before. Beneath the image was the caption,

"Professor Bonaventure R. Golding III, Father of the Somatic Kernel"

Sasha scanned through the article and gleaned more information about Dr. Golding's work in fusing human brains and computer processors. Initially designed to help people with various injuries and diseases, the technology was later applied towards the development of unmanned spaceships to guide cargoes of humans into deep space for colonization efforts.

Suddenly, the ground rocked, throwing Pax and Veronica to the ground. Sasha threw her arms around the monitor as they both went crashing to the floor.

Explosions, familiar from just hours before but much louder, echoed all around. Then everything grew suddenly still and quiet. Everyone's ears were ringing, and it was difficult to breathe, as if the air were being sucked out of the atmosphere.

Pax made it to his feet and ran outside.

Toward the edge of the village where the road sloped down into Orneth, Pax saw Möbius hovering over a wall of Chronowarriors ten shoulders across, marching in military style into the village.

"It's Möbius and an army of Chronowarriors. Let's go!"

He had hoped to reconnoiter and develop a strong plan to prepare for Möbius's return. Time had run out, and the OCL had no plan, no real weapons for this type of battle, and no Artifex Temporis to use as a bargaining tool.

Everyone cinched up their armor, grabbed a weapon, and rushed out into the street. Their small band looked toward the horizon and saw an army heading their way. Each time a row of Chronowarriors passed beneath Möbius, a barrier of violet lights flashed and another one appeared. These were the legions they had feared.

As the legions came close, they all came to a military halt, except the first row. This wall of ten titans continued forward, an uncaring expression of destruction identical on each face. Each carried a large scimitar in one hand and a spear in the other. These weapons clearly indicated that their primary mission was no longer to locate the Artifex Temporis but to destroy the OCL. Unfortunately, the numbers of the Order of the Celestial Lotus seemed to be dropping quickly. With Agathi and Isaiah-Jung gone, and Eck off chasing an idea, they were down to only Pax, Veronica, Sören, and Sasha. Four against four-hundred; the odds were rapidly increasing, and not in their favor.

The OCL quickly formed into a semi-circle, with Pax at the central point in front, closest to the approaching robots. Everyone held a spear and had a pike resting on the ground beside them, with the exception of Veronica, who had her bow ready and drawn. She held extra arrows in the same hand with which she held the bow, and even had an arrow clinched between her teeth. They had trained in and studied so many ancient ways of battle and were using a technique from the Spartans, famous for their battle at Thermopylae, where just a few slowed the tide of many.

As the first Chronowarrior towered over their crescent formation, Pax dropped his spear and reached down to grab the pike that lay beside him, planting the base into the ground and raising the blade. Too late to slow its momentum, the robot pressed forward, reaching for Pax, and impaled itself on the pike in the process. Pax stepped backward and watched as the robot tried to press onward. Waving its scimitar and spear wildly in the air, it made no forward progress and finally fell sideways, immobile on the ground.

Each one did the same as the robots reached them. The technique worked flawlessly, but that eliminated only four out of the ten Chronowarriors in this first wave. Veronica was able to take four of the soldiers out of action with arrows, and Pax and Sören each picked off an additional one with their spears.

Pax knelt to retrieve his pike from the downed robot. He glanced up to see if the next ten were headed their way and immediately wished he had not. He saw the waves of violet continue to light up the sky and could not believe the number of Chronowarriors that stood massed before him.

There must have been five thousand of the dopplegängers stretching out across the open area. Pax looked back at the mix of determination and fear splashed across the faces of his friends and knew he had to do his best for them. He freed the pike and picked up his spear. He was filled with pride in these people who stood beside him; even in the very end, they had never given up on each other.

As Pax took his spot once again in the crescent battle formation, preparing for whatever was to come, his thoughts turned to his mother. Seeing her face in his mind washed away all of the fear of death and the fatigue that threatened to overwhelm his aching body. Sadness swelled in his throat at the thought of never seeing his mother again, that she would have to once again deal with the pain of loss as she had with his father. He feared what would become of everyone under the rule of Möbius.

As the next wall of soldiers descended upon them, scimitars raised, Pax heard a low hum from behind and felt the hair rise on his arms and the back of his neck.

The Chronowarriors before him froze and crumpled to the ground before the OCL. Now twenty more advanced closer behind.

Pax turned and saw Eckhardt standing up on a cart on which some sort of large turbine was mounted like the harpoon gun of an ancient whaling ship. Eck straddled the turbine, which swiveled side to side. Pax could tell the machine was very heavy; Eckhardt was visibly straining to wield the strange device.

Pax heard the sputtering of a generator running close by.

"The electromagnet!" Eck shouted. "I made a few modifications!"

Pax shook his head. He was once again amazed by the young man's brilliance. He had used the large electromagnet that he had developed several years back to help locate metallic building materials underneath the soil. It had originally been just a glorified metal detector, and there was no telling exactly what Eck had done to change it, but it seemed to be working. Hope filled Pax once again and renewed his strength.

Stepping over the downed carcasses of their fallen brethren, the Chronowarriors marched up to the Order of the Celestial Lotus front line once again. With another yelp from Eck and another tingling pulse, this group dropped just as quickly. After a relatively short time, a reef of incapacitated Chronowarriors grew in front of them to the point that all Pax could see was Möbius hovering in the distance.

As the largest battalion yet crested the summit of the Chronowarrior scrap pile, Pax heard no yelp and felt no pulse from behind.

Turning, he saw Eckhardt leaping from the cart as a group of the robots lifted one side, toppling the cart over. The electromagnet broke free and crumpled into pieces, parts strewn across the ground. The generator was still sputtering as the chassis of the cart flipped upside down. A small plume of smoke rose up from beneath, followed by a burst of flame.

Pax guessed that the glass tank holding the alcohol for the generator had cracked and that the alcohol had ignited as it spilled out onto the hot cylinder head. Almost immediately, the whole area was raging in flames. Pax looked away from the billowing black smoke, back toward the approaching Chronowarriors.

They were now completely surrounded by the robots.

CHAPTER SIXTEEN
(Into the belly of the beast)

Rushing out of the elevator as it slowed toward its nadir, Hague quickly scanned the area. They stood in what appeared to be a large natural cavern. Enormous stalactites of luminescent amethyst and cobalt descended from the lofty ceiling. The natural path of the cavern was evident, fading into darkness in one direction and curving quickly out of view in the other. Rough tunnels radiated out in three different directions, unnatural, hewn from explosives and supported in critical areas by large structural beams. Heaps of rock lined the area, and various stockpiles of equipment and supplies peppered the great basin. Stalagmites occasionally rose up from the floor, and many stumps remained of those that had been broken off or leveled with heavy equipment.

Yellow light streamed throughout the space, radiating from large glass fixtures suspended about halfway up the walls. These cup-shaped light housings also hung from the ceilings of the tunnels, trailing off out of sight.

The three interlopers divided the main area and split up to search for explosives or anything else they could use, agreeing to meet in the middle in no more than ten minutes. The area seemed clear of any security, but they wanted to keep close tabs on each other just in case. As they walked, the fine gray dust that permeated everything down here wafted up and hung in the stagnant air.

Dhaal moved tentatively, not confident that he would recognize anything technological that would help, fearing he would miss some critical item that could be used to bring down the reactor.

Agathi attacked the nearest row of shelves, hastily pulling away the black plastic drape that concealed them and casting it aside. Ashen loess dust billowed up and enveloped Agathi, sending her into a coughing fit. Tears came to her eyes as she doubled over and grabbed onto her knees to keep from blacking out. She saw yellow and red stars flashing before her eyes as she stood upright.

Across the chamber, Hague saw Agathi pull off the cover and end up hidden within a cloud of dust; he opted to proceed more cautiously. Gently lifting the protective covering to allow the light to enter, he perused the shelves. On the second shelf, he found a rack of enormous flares mounted onto launchers obviously scaled to fire from the shoulder of a Chronowarrior; it was like an old bazooka-style weapon he had seen in images somewhere in his past. Thinking they could be trapped down in these caverns without any light after they damaged the reactor, he threw one of these flares over his shoulder. After finding nothing else useful on the next several shelves, he finally came across a series of three large containers hidden beneath a dusty tarp.

Gently pulling all three of these cases out, Hague began to open each one. The first two contained soft foam full of long cylindrical holes intended to cushion a series of items, but were completely empty.

The third container revealed what it was intended to protect, as well as what Hague and the others were looking for: explosives.

Hague recognized the digital keypad as the device for operating the detonator; as he had used them before to blast out tunnels in the upper area to create storage and manufacturing space. Designed to hold sixteen of these long canisters, the case now held only three. Hague decided that if these were properly placed, they could inflict significant damage upon the reactor.

He called Agathi and Dhaal over and showed them what he had found. Carefully sliding the first of the cylinders out of the case, Hague exposed the bright red fuselage of the flightless explosive. They stood staring at unfamiliar characters forming words which they could not comprehend. Hague spread the devices out on the floor. Each was just over a meter long and uniform in diameter, except for the digital keypad on one end and a sharp cone at the other, surrounded by a series of four cantilevered appendages. Hague recalled that the conic end was forced into a hole bored into the rock and that the four arms were adjusted to keep the explosive cylinders level against the uneven rock walls.

Agathi gently knelt down and picked one up. It was heavy, but manageable.

"I can carry one," she said, looking up at Hague.

"Great, I'll grab the other two," Hague replied. He would have preferred to carry all three just in case something went wrong. "Let's head back up to the reactor."

Hague knelt down to pick up the two cylinders when a shadow leapt out of the nearby tunnel. The sound of crunching gravel quickly followed.

Hague jumped to his feet, cursing himself for not being more observant. They had assumed that all of the robots were topside, and Hague had been lax in watching out for danger.

As all three looked into the mouth of the tunnel, they saw a large drill bit come into view around the bend. Designed for boring into stone, the bit was a series of three cutters attached in the center and opening outward like the mouth of a steel lamprey searching for food. Jagged teeth bristled, pitted and broken from their constant biting into the dense, hard stone.

Mounted onto a low carriage with steel treads, the machine was being guided by the robots. At some time in the past, the tool had been painted a bright orange color. Now, flecks and patches of the orange paint were still visible, but the overall machine was bare metal, having been well-used and poorly maintained.

Hague counted three robots. One was positioned directly behind the drill, apparently steering the unit. Two other robots stood on one side helping to support a bundle of large rusty pipes that rested on a metal rack suspended from the side of the drill.

As the robots rounded the corner, they immediately spotted the trio of humans standing in the opening of the tunnel and moved forward quickly. Although the drill was weathered, it apparently functioned well and jumped into action, not slowing the advance of the robots at all.

Hague picked up two of the cylinders and ran back to the opposite side of the cavern, depositing them behind one of the covered shelves. He did not want to have these damaged, as the explosives might be their only chance to ever rid themselves of these robots by destroying their power source. The robots were very close by the time he got back. Agathi stood holding the third explosive and he took it from her.

"Run!" Hague shouted. But it was too late. The robots were moving faster than anyone had gauged and were almost on top of them, the drill now spinning wildly and producing a shrill drone. The robot had chosen Agathi as a primary target and was headed directly for her. She stepped back to turn and run but tripped over the empty plastic case that had held the explosives. She fell backward, landing hard on her rear. Her head hit one of the shelves behind her. She winced loudly.

The spinning drill bore down and was within feet of the dazed Agathi when it bucked up and down, no longer advancing. Hague saw that the same case Agathi had tripped over was wedged into the tracks of the drill. The two other robots were pulling back on the bundle of pipe attached to the drill, trying to help the treads regain traction.

The case that was wedged beneath the treads and impeding the drill's progress finally gave way and collapsed under the weight of the drill, allowing the machine to lurch forward.

Hague set the cylinder down as gently as possible and turned back to help Agathi.

From the opposite side, Dhaal sprang out of nowhere. Using his newfound strength, he drove his shoulder hard into the advancing machine, just behind the spinning bit.

The robot controlling the machine lost its grip. The drill spun in a broad arc to the left. Hague had to duck quickly to avoid being struck. Rising up after the drill had moved overhead, he saw the cuirass laying on the ground to Agathi's left, the gauge so dim it was barely visible.

Hague moved toward Agathi; he planned to first pull her out of harm's way and then to grab the cuirass. Continuing to circle around, the whirling bit first hit the robot to the closest to the front of the drill, severing its arm and then completely disintegrating the torso. Shards of metal, plastic, and glass filled the air, striking Hague sharply and pushing him back. Pain seared in the back of the arm that he had raised to protect his face, and he felt shrapnel biting into his exposed forehead and chest.

The driver reacted to the approaching drill bit and dove down to his left, knocking the third robot down in the process. Hague reached up to try and catch the steering wheel of the drill, but the controls were placed very high to accommodate the height of the robots. As he saw the steering controls pass just out of his reach, another pair of hands entered his view and seized the grips. Hague's eyes were blurry from the blood that ran down from the cuts on his forehead and face, and he strained to make out who had taken control, but could not.

The mysterious figure thrust the controls upwards, driving the spinning bit down onto the two remaining robots that flailed on the ground.

Compared to the rock for which the bit was designed to crush, the construction of the robots offered no resistance. More scraps of various materials showered the cavern as the drill annihilated the last two robots.

As Hague blinked to clear his vision, he saw too late that the corselet was trapped underneath the crumpled carcass of one of the robots. As he started to raise his voice, he saw the bit grind into the cuirass before the words could escape his throat.

Hague turned to see Dhaal still face down on the ground and noticed a dark patch spreading across his shoulder.

The whine of the drill thankfully began to fade, and the spiraling bit gradually came to a stop.

In the absence of the shrill screech of the drill, Hague heard footsteps rapidly approaching from the same tunnel from which the robots had appeared. Looking quickly for another weapon with which to confront the robots, he relaxed as he saw Agathi trot from the opening.

Hague had not even seen her leave.

"Isaiah-Jung!" Agathi shrieked in surprise and ran over to the tall, gangly young man now standing in their midst. "How did you get here? When?" she demanded.

"I don't know how I got here," Isaiah-Jung said, shaking his head, still confused. "Probably the same way you did. Möbius was in Orneth, demanding the Artifex Temporis. We were executing an attack. The next thing I knew, Möbius grabbed me, and here I am."

"Hi Isaiah-Jung. I'm Hague, Pax's father," Hague said, extending his hand.

"Pax's dad? I can't believe it. I thought you were dead," Isaiah-Jung stared in disbelief. He threw his arms around Hague and hugged him tightly. "I can't believe it," was all he could say.

"Thank you for your help with the robots, Isaiah," Hague managed to say, despite Isaiah-Jung's crushing hold on him. "I'm not sure how things would have ended if you hadn't showed up."

"Don't thank me," said Isaiah-Jung. "Thank Jukka."

"Jukka?" both Hague and Agathi said in unison. Everyone looked around for another person.

"Yeah," Isaiah-Jung said. "You guys remember him from Orneth, the really tall older man; the climber that disappeared years back. Lucky for me, he found me before those giant robots did."

"He must be the one that pulled me out from in front of the drill." Agathi said. "He pulled me back into that tunnel and told me to wait there. Then he went further down into the passage. I knew there was something familiar about him. But where was he going?"

As if on cue, the elderly man came jogging out of the tunnel, breathing heavily. "There are more robots coming," he said. "There are a lot of them and they're getting close."

"Agathi, take Jukka and help Dhaal to the elevator," Hague told them.

"It's good to see you Jukka," Hague said clapping his shoulders. Hague was guessing that Jukka must be in his late eighties by now, and was amazed how fit and strong he looked. "We have some catching up to do after we get out of this."

Jukka smiled and nodded his head.

"How many robots are there?" Hague asked.

"Hundreds," Jukka replied.

Hague took the flare from off of his shoulder and handed it to the elderly man. "This doesn't weigh much. Give it to Dhaal, maybe he can use it as a crutch."

Agathi moved quickly to Dhaal's side. He was thankfully already starting to stir and had raised himself up onto his side with his left arm. Blood saturated his green robe and he had a large, dark bruise developing on his forehead. As she and Jukka helped him to his feet, she saw Hague run ahead of them carrying two of the cylinders into the elevator.

"You saved my life," Agathi said to Dhaal after seeing that he looked all right. "Thank you."

"You're welcome. Let's call ourselves even." Dhaal smiled faintly and then grimaced as he took another step toward the elevator.

Isaiah-Jung followed Hague as he moved back to the entrance of the tunnel. Hague picked up the last remaining cylinder and asked Isaiah-Jung to hold it level for him.

"Let me know when you're at the elevator," he called to Agathi. He was punching some keys on the digital keypad at the end of the red tube.

Agathi helped Dhaal into the elevator and leaned him against the wall, making sure he could support himself using one of the rails.

Jukka handed Dhaal the flare gun, which he draped over his good shoulder. Agathi then stepped out and signaled to Hague.

Hague waved and then pressed another button on the cylinder.

"Why don't you join them in the elevator, Isaiah? I'll be there shortly," Hague said as he gently lifted the cylinder from Isaiah-Jung's arms. With that, he turned and ran into the opening and out of sight.

From inside the elevator, Agathi saw Hague enter the tunnel and panicked. She made sure Dhaal was all right and then headed for the tunnel herself. Almost as soon as she stepped from the elevator car, Hague came shooting out of the tunnel like a rocket. He swerved over behind the wreckage of the drill and out of sight for a few seconds, and then came bounding over a pile of debris, sprinting toward the elevator, carrying something in his hand.

"Get in the elevator! Head for the reactor!" he yelled.

She turned back and ran. Agathi and Hague hit the elevator at about the same time. Agathi located the indicator for the reactor's floor and pressed the button.

Nothing happened.

She slammed her fist against the button again and the car began to move.

"We'd better sit down and brace ourselves," Hague said, taking Dhaal by the uninjured shoulder.

Seconds after they began their ascent, a thunderous explosion from the cavern below rocked the elevator. The car pitched sideways at an odd angle and seemed to hang there before shakily continuing upward. Another tremor threw Dhaal once again to the floor and slammed Agathi and Jukka against the wall. The lights blinked and then went out. The elevator came to a complete halt.

They all sat in complete darkness. The light from the cuirass had completely failed and offered no aid.

Hague had been knocked to the side and had fallen against Dhaal. Isaiah-Jung helped him as he scrambled up, feeling his way around the floor of the car for the two cylinders.

"Is everyone okay?" he asked.

"I'm fine," said Agathi.

"I'm all right," said Isaiah-Jung.

"I'm fine as well," Dhaal responded, but he didn't sound particularly convincing.

A dim glow filled the car; Jukka had activated a small flashlight on his belt.

"I gather you used one of the explosives to stop the robots?" Jukka inquired, holding up the remaining two cylinders.

"Oh, thank goodness you have those. I was afraid we'd lost them," Hague said reaching for the explosives, "Yeah, I had to use one to seal off that tunnel; there were far more robots than we could fend off.

"I think we can still do plenty of damage to the reactor with these two."

Lights flickered and then came fully to life, and the elevator began to crawl upward again. It seemed to Agathi that they were now moving at a glacial pace. Her excitement and fear from their recent encounter with the mining robots below, combined with her apprehension about carrying such powerful explosives, made the walls of the lift begin to seem like they were closing in on her. Beads of sweat appeared on her forehead, and her breath was shallow and rapid.

Fearing the robotic soldiers had returned to the Chronomicon and were streaming into their lair above, making their way further toward the reactor, made the five very anxious.

Hague had grabbed the cuirass on his way out of the tunnel. He thought it had been totally destroyed by the drill, but had noticed a faint glimmer of light when emerging from the tunnel. The bulk of the breastplate had been macerated by the drill, but miraculously, the gauge remained intact. He hoped this was enough.

The elevator finally arrived at the reactor level. As the five exited the elevator car hauling their dangerous cargo, they heard the voices echoing from above.

"Those are the voices of the humans, but not the sounds of joy," Hague commented.

"They're returning," Dhaal referred to the robot soldiers, stating what everyone feared.

The mixture of distant shouts and yelling resounded within the confines of where they stood and grew louder. These sounds intermingled in an eerie and unnatural way with the mechanical sounds emanating from the cooling systems of the reactor itself.

"We've got to hurry," Hague said, handing the remains of the breastplate to Agathi. "All of you wait here while I go set these charges."

He moved quickly toward the large onion-shaped profile of the structure that housed the core of the reactor. A large hemispherical area protruded from the main housing and was capped by a door with multiple wheels controlling the locking mechanisms. This extrusion was clearly designed to accommodate the height of one of the robots entering the reactor's core for maintenance and repair. Hague speculated that the robots would not be at all concerned about the effect of the intense radiation. For any of the humans to enter the reactor would be suicide. It would be equally catastrophic if they were still present when these explosives were detonated or if the soldiers found them there.

Light filtering through a heavy glass panel on a door caught Hague's attention as he moved toward the reactor. His heart leapt as he peered through the panel.

"Isaiah-Jung! Jukka! Come quick!" Hague called back.

The two men arrived to see Hague emerging from a chamber, his arms loaded with the copper breastplates, the dials on each glowing brightly.

"Looks like we caught a break," Hague said, "Take these and grab as many more as you can. Ask Dhaal how they work, then take them to the men above and tell them what to do. If Dhaal is correct, they can cluster together in groups and use these to return home. Tell them to hurry."

Hague picked up one of the cylinders from the floor and began working to attach it onto the metal wheel centered on the door leading into the reactor. The cantilevered arms on the explosive easily grasped the spokes on the wheel. Hague stood up and cautiously pressed down on the device, checking that it was firmly attached before completely letting go.

Hague picked up the last remaining cylinder and moved around the base of the reactor. Studying the structure, he determined that the pipes before him served to channel the water from the pool above and into a series of large spiral turbines, each housed in an elongated glass cylinder. Hague concluded that these turbines forced the water into the cooling system of the reactor. Adjacent to the point where the turbines flowed into the reactor was a larger tube that split up into several smaller pipes, each snaking out and coiling into convoluted nests of tubing before joining once again into the larger tube almost fifty meters away. This tube surged skyward and provided a channel for the superheated water to flow back out into the pool above where it could cool before cycling through again.

The glass turbines seemed like the weakest points in the overall system. Hague began to attach the second explosive device to a large flange at the end of a turbine closest to the reactor. If this section of the cooling system were destroyed, the cool water would spill out before it ever made it to the reactor's core. In no time at all after that, the reactor would overheat and either shut down or breach the reactor barriers. In either scenario, there was no reactor, no generator, and no power for the robots.

Hague thought briefly of what might happen if he set both of these charges and then they could not escape. He concluded that since either being recaptured by Möbius or being incinerated in a nuclear meltdown both equated to death, that he would take his chances with the explosives. He was driven to get back to Orneth to see his wife and son, as well as to help all those people who had been held prisoner here, and believed with all his heart that this was indeed the best course of action.

Hague activated the timer on the explosive device.

"We've got to get out of here," he said, emerging from the nest of pipes and tubing that filled this place. "We'll be sitting ducks in the elevator; our only way out is the stairs."

"You forgot about these," said Agathi. She held the ragged shards of the cuirass that Hague had rescued in one hand, and a shiny new one in the other. Hague could see the gauges on both radiating brilliant white light.

CHAPTER SEVENTEEN
(Deus Ex Machina)

Pax turned to face an array of glistening scimitars waving through the air, bearing down upon him. Fighting valiantly with a broken pike, he downed several more of the menacing Chronowarriors before having to retreat a few precious steps. Now, the remains of the OCL were forced into a tight circle, elbow to elbow, with nowhere left to run. Pax thrust at an approaching robot and felt what remained of the well-worn hickory shaft splinter from the blunt force. The blade of the pike cut deeply and now jutted out of the Chronowarrior's midsection, but the robot kept advancing nevertheless. Pax tossed the remnant scrap of the pike's shaft to the ground.

Standing completely unarmed, Pax loosened the strap of his helmet and removed it. He planned to hurl it at the oncoming attacker when it drew nearer. There had been no thought of a plan beyond such a desperate act, but Pax doubted that he had much time remaining anyway.

Sweat-soaked hair fell across his face, and he stole a glance around to see how the rest of the team fared. To Pax, time seemed to almost stop. Seconds became minutes as he surveyed the scene, a scene of combat that had been played out so many times over the history of the world. He wondered if this sensation of time was common for the last precious few seconds of each person's life.

To his left, Sasha fought fiercely with a robot using a scimitar that she had liberated from the wrecked Chronowarrior at her feet. The downed robot's severed arm jutted upward, twisted at a bizarre angle.

Taking inspiration from Sasha, Pax threw his helmet at the robot that was now nearly upon him, and then dove to his left to reach for a scimitar from another fallen automaton. As he rolled over a heap of Chronowarriors, he heard a loud crack as his helmet struck its target. He knew well enough that the glass cylinder hidden within the stoic mask of the robot had shattered. The now familiar odor of the mysterious blue fluid filled the air.

Pax's hand found the hilt of a sword, and he was up on his feet in a flash and once again in the fray. Reaching deep down inside, he found strength where he thought none remained. In a powerful and sweeping arc, he struck the robot mid-torso, completely cutting the staggering Chronowarrior in half. A spray of gears and springs erupted from the severed body cavity and rained down all around Pax and the robot. Seconds later, the quivering legs of the damaged robot collapsed into an inanimate heap. The irony of having destroyed his attacker with one of the Chronowarriors' own weapons did not escape Pax.

Veronica had long since exhausted her supply of arrows, and valiantly whirled a morning star over her head. Her long henna ponytail swung in unison with the sharp metal blade. Sunlight glinted off both the blade and the golden weights at the end of her hair. She looked exhausted, but Pax doubted that she would ever succumb to her fatigue. Their eyes connected briefly on one of her rotations, and he saw a tight smile on her lips. She winked before her face spun out of sight and she decapitated a nearby attacker. A spray of blue fluid filled the air as the giant crumpled to the ground, only to have his spot filled by another.

Beyond Veronica, Pax could see several of the robots engulfed in flames, moving erratically around the area. Eckhardt was surrounded by a group of Chronowarriors, one of which was charred and smoldering.

Veronica and Sören were now forced back to back, Veronica still spinning the morning star over her head and Sören swinging his crossbow like a club. As Pax watched, a Chronowarrior brought its scimitar down on Sören. He instinctively raised the stock of the crossbow in defense and was driven to the ground, the crossbow splintering. Veronica shattered the right shoulder of the robot, rendering it useless. Sören freed the sword from its wrecked arm and drove it into the torso of the robot to the sound of grinding gears and the shriek of metal on metal. Both Veronica and Sören turned to parry more advancing robots.

Möbius loomed on the near horizon, hovering over the still advancing waves of his army. Writhing legs splayed out, spiderlike; an eerie black profile eclipsed the sunlight beyond. As Pax watched, Möbius disappeared over the horizon.

Pax turned and was startled that a Chronowarrior towered over him, having advanced quickly while he had been distracted by Möbius. Pax cursed himself for being caught unawares; the robot stood so close that Pax could not even raise the scimitar that dangled at his side. He tried to step backward, but was blocked by a heap of lifeless robots.

With the cold, glistening crescent of its scimitar poised high above, ready to come slicing down onto Pax, the robot stopped. Pax glared up into the glowing synthetic eyes of the robot, defiantly staring upward in a posture of pride, his fatigued mind scrambling for a plan of action. Expecting the end, with his heart beating up into his throat, his heartbeat began to slow slightly as the robot's pause stretched on. Eventually, the entire robot teetered, the white light in the cold eyes went dark, and the giant went crashing backward. Still clinging to the scimitar and holding the blade firmly overhead within its massive hands, the Chronowarrior showed no signs of life.

Pax moved to knock the scimitar from the grip of the fallen robot. In his peripheral sight, he saw many of the robots crashing to the ground. The legions of those still upright were completely immobile.

Eckhardt emerged from the cage of inanimate soldiers that encircled him.

Sasha continued to hack at a downed Chronowarrior with the giant scimitar, either not yet realizing that they were all now inoperable or not wanting to risk them coming back to life.

Veronica sat on the ground with her face buried in her hands. Pax walked over and sat down beside her.

One by one, the all made their way over, stripping off parts of their armor and letting it fall to the ground.

A sudden flash of light startled everyone and sent them scrambling to retrieve armor or locate a weapon, fearing that another wave of Chronowarriors was arriving.

Agathi, Dhaal, Isaiah-Jung, and two men no one recognized now stood clustered in their midst.

Everyone was elated to see the missing members of their team safely back with them. Veronica jumped quickly to her feet ran to Agathi and wrapped her tightly in a hug. Pax threw his arm around Dhaal, cautious of his visibly damaged shoulder. Relief and joy were clearly visible on all their faces, despite all the dirt, dried blood, and bruises. Each one wondered how much more fight they could have mustered should more Chronowarriors have arrived.

"Welcome back," Pax said, clasping Dhaal's good shoulder and moving to hug Agathi. "I was afraid we would never see you again. I am going to guess that you were fighting a battle of your own, helping us out here at the same time," Pax said, smiling through the fatigue.

Pax turned to Hague. The man seemed strangely familiar to him and was looking far more intently at Pax than a typical stranger, probing every feature of his face, looking for something specific. Haggard and exhausted, he seemed at the same time to convey a contagious sense of hopeful energy.

Pax paused, deeply returning the man's stare. He heard Agathi saying the name Jukka, but everything around him was fading away and then all he could see was Hague before him. As the cloth draping a distant memory fell away, a connection fell into place. At first Pax fought such a memory, afraid to allow any false hope to seep through any fissures in the wall that contained his deepest hopes and dreams. He fought it, but the connection became too strong and the dam broke away, and the memory that was not a memory filled his consciousness.

Tears streamed from Hague's eyes as if in unison with the deluge of genetic connections taking place in Pax's psyche.

The two emotionally embraced without a word.

"Pax, it's me. It's your father." Hague realized they were both aware of this, but he just wanted to hear the words out loud.

Veronica burst into tears once again, sobbing loudly with joy for Pax. A beautiful smile spread across Sasha's face, now visible as she undid the chain mail that had protected her. Her white teeth glowed, contrasted against her filthy cheeks and the sweaty black hair pasted against her face. She reached up and grabbed her helmet by the black horns that jutted upwards, pulling it from her head.

Veronica, Sasha, Agathi, Sören, Isaiah-Jung, and Eckhardt all migrated over to Pax and his father.

"I knew you were alive," Pax said, finally releasing his father's grip enough to stare into his face. "I knew you'd come back some day."

"I've dreamt of this day," Hague finally managed. "That dream is what's kept me alive. Let's go find Isolde; let's go see your mother. We're a family once again."

"We always were," Pax choked, embracing his father once again and hugging him so tightly, as if trying to make up for years of having missed the opportunity as a child.

"We have to make sure that all of the men that Möbius captured make it back to their families," Hague said. "We can't leave anyone behind."

"We'll make sure Dad. We will."

"Möbius is coming back," Sören interjected, pointing toward the horizon. Möbius swept back and forth over the inanimate Chronowarriors, spewing commands in a language unintelligible to anyone, his shape growing larger with each passing second. In no time at all, Möbius was hovering in the air before them.

The group pulled together defensively, not sure what to expect from Möbius without his army.

"I will return to claim what is mine. You have not seen the last of me!" Möbius bellowed.

"I am ..." was all that the group heard before Möbius was drowned out by a loud blast. A stream of dense smoke and fire trailed over their heads and quickly traced a path to Möbius, erupting in a cloud of flame.

The group turned to see Dhaal standing behind them with the flare gun that Hague had found in the bowels of the Chronomicon. Smoke seethed from the launcher.

A thunderous boom echoed out, returning their attention to Möbius. Spinning wildly out of control, Möbius was engulfed in a blistering white light. Showers of sparks and flame sprayed outward in a spiral array, glowing brightly before softly falling to the earth and fading out, extinguished.

Ribbons a white smoke swirled about and created the illusion of a cage that held Möbius contained within.

The creature finally stabilized and turned to face the Order of the Celestial Lotus. Many of his tentacles were visibly burnt and blistered and flailed about erratically. A layer of soot covered the glass dome, making the unblinking eye within only dimly visible.

"I will return!" Möbius barked, clearing away an area on the ovoid with the sweep of a hand, the spinning eyes now clearly directed at the group, radiating hatred.

"Rest assured that the Artifex Temporis will be mine once again. Your days are numbered!"

Blackened and smoking, Möbius turned and swam quickly away from them through the air, disappearing into a final violet flash of light.

CHAPTER EIGHTEEN
(Apocalypse)

Smoke and debris billowed high into the dark sky, forming a monument of destruction over the Chronomicon. A blood-red glow emanated from within the mushroom cloud and cast an unnatural, paranormal glow over the desolate basin.

Möbius hovered at the core of the plume of destruction, basking in the intense heat of the radiation that spewed from the ruptured core of the reactor below. Raw energy flowed into his damaged tentacles, which hung suspended within the radioactive steam that violently roiled up from the fissure in the chasm's surface.

Revolving madly, the eyes stared out into infinity, the mind within contemplating structural improvements and scheming nefarious plans against the Order of the Celestial Lotus.

He was mentally grimacing at the thought of the OCL and their ability to humiliate him and thwart his plans. However inferior these humans might be as compared to his own superiority, he knew they would protect the Artifex Temporis at all cost. Möbius doubted that their small finite minds would ever comprehend the true power of the Artifex or discern its operation. Should they discover how to control the device, they would be a powerful force, but they had held the Artifex for years and were apparently more concerned with its protection than its function.

The humans' folly was the only thing preventing Möbius's plans for the power of universal hegemony, a temporary ripple in his plans that spanned eternity. He had been too cautious in his approach and would not make the same mistakes again. Möbius's return would be swift and unexpected, catching the puny and weak Order of the Celestial Lotus completely by surprise. They had benefited from their luck and the fact that Möbius had underestimated human ingenuity. The humans' luck had now run out.

Surveying the Chronomicon, Möbius moved into the ruined cavern and headed directly for the chambers that housed the ÜberSoldiers. The dull metal exterior of the closest silo was crumpled, and a visible breach gaped like an opened wound near the top. The blackness within the tear was like blood waiting to spill out. A sense of panic filled Möbius as he raced toward the tower and attacked the large yellow wheel on the outside of the bulkhead, straining to free the manual release on the massive door.

The wheel finally moved, and the heavy door swung outward slowly before completely coming off of the hinges and crashing to the ground. Möbius cautiously peered inside and examined the monstrous machines. Three times the size of an inferior Chronowarrior, each was driven by its own internal reactor and designed for more intense action in far more combative and hostile areas of the universe. Möbius now regretted his oversight in not using these few ÜberSoldiers to quickly deal with the humans.

Each colossus filled the silo and stood statuesque, immobile. Möbius had abandoned any thoughts of a human façade for these amazing machines, instead striving to highlight the beauty of their mechanical function and form.

He now saw the failure in the design of the legions of Chronowarriors remotely powered by a single power source. This could be corrected by outfitting each unit with its own power supply, but would that be enough? Could they still be useful? Möbius now saw the Chronowarriors as weak, legions defeated by the tenacity of the humans and their uncharacteristic foresight in thinking to target the reactor. Möbius was already developing plans to use the ÜberSoldiers to begin retrieving the thousands of helpless Chronowarriors, while he focused on repairs to the central reactor. Even if he opted to scrap the Chronowarriors and use their weak carcasses for parts, he did not want them littering the plains around Orneth where they would serve as a monument to his loss. Neither did he want those inferior humans snooping around and studying his engineering; even in defeat, the Chronowarriors represented far superior design and engineering than anything currently in use by that primitive lot.

Images of the future exploded across a fevered consciousness: detailed designs of how Möbius would enhance his army and himself.

"Physician, heal thyself!" he screamed.

"I will," he answered himself, his voice shrill and cracking; the voice of madness.

Möbius envisioned enhancements to his own armor and the addition of powerful weaponry to his chassis. "The Chronowarriors cannot be salvaged. They will be destroyed," he whispered decisively.

The concepts flooding into his conscious, merging with calculated physical designs, produced a mélange of impressive and awe-inspiring technology: the technology of dominance and control.

Möbius was reveling in his survival and capitalizing on what he had already learned in defeat.

Möbius now reeled when he considered the flaws and weaknesses of what he had done when compared to these new industrial visions that splattered across his awareness.

The radiation was already changing his organic component, mutating and strengthening his tentacles.

Once he had possession of the Artifex Temporis, he would have the power to reverse the course of history and address his mistakes, leaving Posterity to record his subjugation of the universe as flawless, with the embarrassing encounters with those meddlesome humans omitted, as well as any trace of their history.

Möbius was not even conscious of the unregulated gamma radiation that poured through him, altering anything natural that remained. The reactor had reached critical mass, and the heat approached that of a blazing sun, but that did not approach the heat of the obsessive desire that burned within the mind of Möbius. He knew that he must have control of the Artifex Temporis.

Möbius would then have all the time in the world—literally.

Made in the USA
Lexington, KY
02 December 2010